Fontana Dam - Sluice Release - From Official TVA Photos

FONTANA

"Based on Clandestine Events before and after WWII"

by

Ian Feldman

SSI Publishing, LLC

P.O. Box 815

Holly Springs, GA 30142

USA

Copyright 2024 © Ian Feldman

This Book is a work of Fiction. Names, characters, businesses, organizations, places, events, incidents are the product of the author's imagination or are used fictitiously. Any resemblance to actual persons, living or dead or locales is entirely coincidental.

Cover Design adapted from Getty Images (hand and gun).

Table of Contents

EPIGRAPH

PROLOGUE

PART ONE: The Present - October

Chapter 1: THE SLUICE
Chapter 2: MONROE VANN

PART TWO: The Agency Emerges

Chapter 3: ALSOS
Chapter 4: MAG PARABELLUM
Chapter 5: WKNX TV NEWS
Chapter 6: THE CHEROKEE NATION CASINO
Chapter 7: THE WKNX NEWS ANCHOR
Chapter 8: ONWARD TO FONTANA
Chapter 9: CHEROKEE NC
Chapter 10: CRAPS TABLE TIME

Chapter 11: THE CLUB

PART THREE: The Final Folly

Chapter 12: THE INTERVIEW

Chapter 13: THE SHAMAN'S CABIN

Chapter 14: AWINITA VAN

Chapter 15: THE UTILITY BUILDING REVEAL

Chapter 16: ANDERSON'S WARNING

Chapter 17: THE CITATION XLS

Chapter 18: THE RECKONING

PART FOUR: Escape into Vapor

Chapter 19: FLIGHT TO PARADISE

Chapter 20: A VILLA ON BONAIRE

EPIGRAPH

NAGASAKI, JAPAN – AUGUST 9, 1945

"*A mushroom cloud forms in vast cloud layers and glows white-hot over the last major city on our planet, to ever experience a nuclear attack on humankind. Thousands of people are vaporized and thousands more are left burning in the incendiary aftermath of the horror.*

Fat Man, a nuclear implosion bomb, the second Atomic Bomb created by the United States Manhattan Project, has at last expended its power of twenty-thousand plus tons of TNT on an unsuspecting enemy."

PROLOGUE

A clandestine ALSOS Operations Center near Washington, DC:

Jack Wolcott stares at his keyboard, as he prepares to type his report.

He muses his thoughts in secret images before typing.

"Only a limited few people in the World know of ALSOS. But since its inception in 1943, during the Manhattan Project, ALSOS has been a super-secret agency on the hunt for Nuclear Rogue Nations and those vile Leaders that create and proliferate Nuclear Devices for War and Human mass destruction.

In March 2007, Israeli intelligence agents assisted me and my tech expert YUAN, in Vienna, Austria, with a break-in to the offices of Syria's atomic energy director.

Once in place, Yuan secretly downloaded the entire contents of their secure computer."

Secret images suddenly appear clearly in Jack's mind.

VIENNA, AUSTRIA – 2007

SYRIAN EMBASSY - SECRET INNER OFFICE - NIGHT

Two men in black ninja gear slip silently out of an overhead vent-return, then drop into the room - one goes to a dormant computer - starts it and inserts a high tech flash drive - the screen ignites, flowing with massive amounts of data, as all of it seems to suck back into the high tech flash drive.

Their faces are covered, as one of the men in black ninja gear, quickly types code into the computer, then returns it to its dormant state, as he removes the high tech flash drive - the other operative meticulously cleans the room, then swiftly, they both move back up into the air duct system and disappear.

"It was then that ALSOS and Israel discovered that Syria was just weeks away from completing a nuclear reactor, with the help of Iran and North Korea. It was located at a place called Eir al-Zour near the Euphrates River in Syria.

This fact created an urgent, massive threat to Israel - not only that, but it was almost in Israel's backyard, just over the Northern border with Syria.

But BUSH and the United States along with NATO, stood by powerless to react - so we were sent by ALSOS, to step in and once again eliminate the Terrorist Snake."

Then another image suddenly appears in Jack's mind.

SYRIAN DESERT

WEST OF EIR AL-ZOUR - SUNSET

Four Israeli F-15 and F-16 fighter jets streak like laser bullets flying low into Syria across the moonscape desert terrain, then turn eastward, coming out of the blazing sunset toward the Syrian Nuclear reactor. In moments, missiles and multiple two thousand pound bombs explode violently all over the facility as the Israeli fighter jets rapidly return back into the final rays of the setting sun, without any radar or visual detection.

"ALSOS sent me eleven years ago to help Israel with Syria and now I'm back. But this time, it's the Devil's Lair itself, IRAN, 2018.

Israel, The United States and the IAEA, all know Iran's supreme leader, Ayatollah Ali Khamenei, wants Israel "eradicated" - with their OWN nuclear weapons once they are operational.

So this is my third visit to Iran and hopefully my last.

First, it was the heavy water reactor at Arak, then Bushir and now Natanz."

Finally, it all becomes crystal clear as the next visual flashes in Jack's mind.

WEST OF NATANZ, IRAN - 2018

IRANIAN DESERT - OUTSIDE NATANZ - SUNSET

A lone Mercedes-Benz G63 AMG SUV, with black-out windows and armor, strides effortlessly across the rocky terrain toward what looks like a concrete bunker then comes to a halt kicking up a small dust plume . . .

AS

MERCEDES-BENZ SUV - AT THE BUNKER

Two Iranian Military Officers exit the rear doors of the vehicle, one with a narrow briefcase.

The man with the briefcase turns to look across the desert for a mental moment, as we see his bearded face - it's JACK himself in disguise, as a High Level Iranian Officer.

INSIDE THE BUNKER

Then quickly, both Operatives enter a hidden trap door.

Jack and his Cyber Operative move smartly throughout a maze of corridors. Only a few security people observe them, but they salute their high rank and then return to their posts.

Finally, an enormous room opens in front of them with banks of computers, stainless steel centrifuges and pipes as far as the eye can see. They move quickly into a headquarters office overlooking the massive bay with several scientists and revolutionary guard bureaucrats looking down at their own computer screens.

Jack stands guard as his Cyber Operative goes directly to a central computer and inserts the high tech Black-Ops flash drive. Waits several seconds then replaces it back into Jack's briefcase.

In ten minutes the ALSOS team is gone.

"That night, my team once again placed the ALSOS version of the STUXNET worm directly into Iran's core centrifuge and reactor computers. While offshore the USS Abraham Lincoln carrier strike group, waited in the Persian Gulf to convey a hard message to Iran, that besides Israel, a credible and massive US deterrent existed at their doorstep.

So short of military force - ALSOS and our STUXNET WORM prevented Iran from getting nuclear weapons for hopefully until a future time."

PART ONE

The Present

October

Chapter 1

THE SLUICE

MOUNTAINS OF NORTH CAROLINA

FONTANA DAM - UPSTREAM LAKE AREA - QUALLA BOUNDARY

We hear the SOUND and FURY of an epic mountain rainstorm as THUNDER, then lightning light-up the night sky revealing a washed out road with RUSHING white-water undermining a large boulder. . .

Looking CLOSER we follow the massive rock as it ERUPTS out of the mountainside, VIOLENTLY rolling downward to a cliff side above a lake. . .

EXPLODING into the water, we track it into the black depths deeper to the ruins of an old mining town called Fontana, and now hidden forever under this massive body of water formed by the Little Tennessee River. . .

A DEEP RUMBLE announces the boulder's destruction of what appears to be a miner cabin. Then suddenly, it CRASHES through a rotted door on the interior floor and FALLS in slow motion into the abyss as. . .

Something hidden for years escapes the captivity of the now destroyed trap door and drifts SILENTLY upward toward the lake's surface . . .

In another view... from this close, ahead, it looks like a desert surface, sand dunes, then canyons, valleys. Dim light shading it perfectly, growing brighter. With a little more detail. More light. A rough surface. Etched. Like scorched arid wasteland. Even wider, now we see it, as the lake water moves forward - a concrete surface. Years of aging from the 1940's in a high altitude sun. As it begins to form...the solid floor of a sluice. It's as wide as a two lane tunnel. Suddenly a trickle of water begins flushing over it. At first only a small stream of water. Concrete is everywhere. Man-made but of enormous magnitude. Steel sluice gates are suddenly raised open by monstrous electric engines as the stream becomes a gushing river of water flowing away from the escarpment lake into the depths of its duel tunnel openings.

The SOUNDS become louder than Niagara Falls as a FURIOUS wall of gushing white-water fills the tunnel from floor to ceiling, while the torrent descends into a dark chasm. Leaves, branches, small trees, thousands of gallons of green mountain lake water trapped in its POWERFUL unrelenting downward surge.

A hazy sunrise throws dappled shadows across the RUSHING water as we see something dark moving on the lake's surface from where the boulder entered. It's moving toward the sluice gates. At first, slowly, then faster, then WHAM, our eyes are focused on the dark object. The object is drawn magnetically to the edge of the massive waterfall GUSHING toward the sluice tunnel. No one else sees it. Then as it rolls over to enter the sluice. Clearly now; a decomposed face stares up at us for a brief moment. Black eye sockets wide open - dull and dead. Its body clothed in rotted fabric FLUSHES past us into a TORRENT of water pouring downward into the abyss of the giant tunnels ending at the base of the dam.

In the early morning, down below the Dam, a young Female Reporter, TRISH FREEMAN for a Knoxville TV news station and her cameraman are filming the uncommon event, a major water release from TVA's enormous four-hundred-foot high Fontana Dam.

15 | Fontana

Blasts of water eject in a ROAR OF SOUND AND FURY as the reporter comments, almost yelling, not to be drowned out by the NOISE of the torrent coming out of the giant pipes.

Trish is in her cameraman's view finder as she speaks . . .

 "This is the biggest Dam east of the Rockies, almost a mile wide. It has been here for over seventy-five years, since The Second World War. The Pentagon and TVA built it for the War effort.

They used ALCOA's Land and they took the additional land they needed from the Sovereign Cherokee Nation. General Groves said they needed more Electricity for the Atom Bomb Project at Oak Ridge as well as to make more Aluminum at ALCOA, Tennessee for B-17 and B-29 production, so the Feds once again used their absolute power.

At this moment, you are watching over fifty-seven thousand gallons of water per second, rush out of these enormous duel pipes."

Water vapor escapes the sluice ejection point and instantly freezes in the air as it causes an ice storm on the trees and any objects in its path, including the camera lens, as it glistens in the early sunlight . . .

"That water is moving at ninety miles an hour as it blasts out of those two tunnels."

When, just forward of her high heels -- EXPLODING --

A FREAKISH Misshapen form -- The decomposed BODY from above, slams into the concrete wall in front of Trish, then flips over onto the gravel she's standing on. Staring up at her. Its black eye sockets wide open. Its body in rotted fabric as . . .

Trish begins SCREAMING insanely.

Chapter 2

MONROE VANN

NEAR FONTANA DAM - CHEROKEE CABIN - QUALLA BOUNDARY

A Native American man, Monroe Vann lies on his back in bed. He is still a solid hunk of tanned flesh in his early fifties, with a full head of rich black hair. On top of him is a much younger Native American woman. We catch flashes of her face for a moment, as she grinds on him from side to side. Now we can see more of her, enough to realize that this is a young beautiful girl, not more than twenty years old.

She moves wildly, grinding her hips into him, her head arched back, her hands holding his muscular legs as Monroe grips her breasts tightly. Suddenly, the girl faces into his eyes and grabs his shoulders as he forces himself deeper inside her.

They move violently -- faster -- and faster.

We slowly realize these two are being filmed by an unmanned 1980's type video camera mounted on a tripod. We are watching the TELEVISION screen as the we PULL BACK even further viewing the full room with the couple in view.

Further back still. We see a solid wood cabin door and pan through a window as two QUALLA POLICE OFFICERS march toward the cabin door.

We look around the room and back to the window.

Rain streaks down the window as -- LIGHTNING flashes outside.

The pounding SOUND of the QUALLA OFFICERS at the door shocks the couple into ACTION as they break away from each other and Monroe grabs a gun holstered by the bed, with a QUALLA Police Chief Star pinned in the belt.

One of the QUALLA POLICE OFFICERS YELLS at the door.

"Chief! Gotta get you up! The SBI's at the Station with a North Carolina Governor and Federal Search Warrant."

Then without response, together both QUALLA POLICE OFFICERS YELL at the door.

"Chief, open up!"

In an instant the door opens with a loud CRASH, as both Officers jump backward. Monroe stands in the doorway in his jockey shorts and hair askew. As we look past him inside.

The young beautiful Native American girl, Doe Angel, stands topless behind him facing the Officers, for all to see.

"What da Hell is goin on!"

"It's One in the Morning, you idiots!

Federal Warrant or No Federal Warrant. . . tell that Government Cavalry Squad to get a room at The Casino Hotel and I'll meet um at Seven in the Morning!

This is The Independent Cherokee Nation and I set the Qualla Council's schedule around here! You got that, Officers!"

Shaken up, as they react to his orders, both Officers salute with a fist to their chests and move backward, then turn to their Jeep.

The first Officer reacts on the Chief's orders.

"Roger Chief! We got that!

They ain't gonna like it, but we'll tell um!"

"See you at the Station, Chief."

CHEROKEE POLICE HQ - NEXT MORNING

Police Chief Vann is fumbling with his Coffee Maker. An unlit cigarette hangs out of this mouth as he adds water to the pot and reacts.

"Dammit! Where's Andrew Black Hawk?"

The sheepish female voice of Doe Angel answers in the background.

"Chief, I can make that for you. There are two SBI Men here at the front desk, waiting for you."

Chief Vann marches into the room, as Angel passes him to make the coffee. He quickly scans the two SBI business suits from Raleigh, but doesn't know them. His cigarette is now lit and his facial muscles intense as he reacts.

"Okay! What's up Gentlemen?"

Quietly, first SBI Officer responds. . .

"Chief Vann, as you know, the State forensics lab verified the DNA of that ancient corpse in your Morgue, it's Native American.

Of course, we did it for you, at no cost."

Quickly, Vann reacts. . .

"Yeah! I appreciate that, too! But what's this State and Federal Search Warrant all about?"

Finally, the first SBI Officer reveals the real reason. . .

"Chief, since the corpse came from within the Dam's Federal TVA Property, the Feds have asked us to be at the autopsy and retrieve any possible bullet fragments."

This time, Vann reacts with aggression. . .

"Damn Feds! So they think he was murdered?"

The first SBI Officer reveals their concern. . .

"Not necessarily, Chief. But murder does fall under our purview.

The FEDS only want bullet fragments, should the Coroner find any."

Vann grins, pissed off.

"They just keep appropriating things from our Cherokee Nation, even now, without any consequences!

They took our lands for that Dam and along with our sacred burial grounds on Eagle Creek."

"Suppose they want his clothes too?"

The SBI Officer tries to calm him.

"Just those fragments, Chief. They sent some heavy weight Federal Attorneys down to Raleigh from DC, yesterday."

"That's why the Judge issued the Warrant. They have jurisdiction."

Vann reacts, agitated.

"Fine! Let me see that Warrant."

The Second SBI Officer pulls out an official envelope and hands Chief Vann the Warrant Document. The Chief intensely scans the Document and checks the Attorney Names along with the Judge, then reacts.

"I know these Guys!

They're all 'White Supremacist Puppets' from that Nazi regime in Washington!"

The SBI Officer looks at him, concerned.

"It's all legal, Chief."

Without acknowledgement, Chief Vann shrugs, then shouts back at Doe Angel.

"Angel! Get Andrew Black Hawk in here, NOW!"

"I'm taking these guys down to the Morgue, so call the Doc and have him open up for us."

Doe Angel shouts back at him.

"Roger, Chief.

But, when you coming back?"

Chief Vann picks up the document and starts for the door as the Officers turn to get a final look at the sexy young Doe Angel, as she sashays back to the doorway of the Front Office. Vann gives her a wink and shouts back!

"No tellin', Angel. No tellin'. Come on Gentlemen,

She'll "Slice your throats", if you look at her too closely!"

Chief Vann grins, as he turns to the stunned SBI Officers.

"Okay Fellas,

Let's cut this Indian open!"

PART TWO

The Agency Emerges

Chapter 3

ALSOS

WASHINGTON STATE

COULEE HQ – ALSOS MAIN HEADQUARTERS

Everything seems to be glowing from indirect lighting as we enter a Top Secret Conference Room. The dark room is lit by a massive VIDEO SCREEN - FULL FRAME, as we meet Thomas Macabe. He's head of a deep secret Agency held over, secretly funded and never closed since the WWII Manhattan Project.

Macabe is standing in some sort of an underground bunker with people silently working at computer monitors in the background. He's agitated and slams down his fist on a table.

No one moves, - everyone in the room is nervously busy around him, avoiding his eyes.

This place is ALSOS MAIN HEADQUARTERS (COULEE HQ) -- a super TOP SECRET Espionage and Assassination Unit within the US ENERGY DEPARTMENT hidden safely underground in the Cascades Mountain Range of Washington State between the Grand Coulee Dam and Hanford's Plutonium Production Z PLANT. It's been operating freely with massive funding, plus FBI, CIA and NSA support at the highest levels, and NO Congressional or Presidential oversight, since WWII. Suddenly, Macabe picks up a headset and begins addressing all present and those on-line, in a deep threatening tone of voice.

"...Are you aware, no, no -- you must be aware

that since the time of General Groves building this Agency, that nothing like this has ever happened.

We are now exposed to the LIGHT and I'm ordering that this mess at Fontana be cleaned up without ANY more, loose ends!

Even our current Federal and State Governments are our enemy in this situation. No one can know what happened THEN, and No one can know who directed it THEN.

All clean-up options are in effect and all results and reports are to me personally within 48 hours.

I want it done and gone -

Is that precise enough, GENERAL!"

The giant monitor screen freezes with Macabe's mouth in a vicious growl, then -

Macabe's Washington DC based ALSOS commander, General Anderson, switches off the remote controlled screen and turns up the room lights in another undisclosed deep cellar of the old AEC, now designated - The Department of Energy.

Six black suited ALSOS underlings face him, intensely sitting around the table, like alligators in a swamp, waiting for the goat to be thrown in.

We scan the faces, but the one we focus on is Jack Wolcott, a nondescript guy, with the powerful physical and mental elements of an assassin hidden beneath his corporate suited exterior. Anderson sees him first as he lets loose. . .

"...Are we CLEAR on the Directors Orders?"

In unison, the six operative shout out!

"CLEAR GENERAL!"

"Okay then!" Anderson reacts.

"You all know your assignments, so let's CLEAN this mess now!"

"And Wolcott, you're on lead with this!

Everyone else, DISMISSED."

Wolcott's face says this is a SURPRISE to him. But his CLOSED FISTS suggest something else. Then, as he stands, his PALMS SOLIDLY GRIP the board room table, waiting for the others to exit first as he speaks up.

"I'll need COMPLETE autonomy on this one, General No outside interference."

"You've got it, Jack! Just keep me updated as you clean it up!"

"Now Go!" Anderson's face has a look of serious concern.

Jack Wolcott exits the room, as suddenly the GIANT screen

RE-IGNITES with Thomas Macabe's image refilling the blank monitor screen.

Macabe looks directly at General Anderson. Long pause.

"...Did you clear the room, Anderson?"

"Yes Sir, we're alone!" Anderson sweats.

"...Once again Anderson, those damn exploding MAG PARABELLUM bullets with God knows how much curare in them, has come back to haunt us!

They were TOP SECRET and advanced tech in the 1940's, and were never to be used in the field again. . . No one in the US or Overseas uses them!

It's a signature killer!

But against my ORDERS your group continues that legacy. It's your obsession with a legacy that your father developed to kill that NAZI Reinhard Heydrich for the Brits."

Macabe pauses for effect.

"And it can only be traced back to ALSOS. . .

You used them in Turkey, you used them in Austria and Iraq, and now they have been exposed again in this FONTANA incident.

How are you going to clean this one up, without the DOD and the FBI finally knowing it was us?"

General Anderson looks at his watch in a quick reaction.

"It's going to be cleaned up, Sir! Jack Wolcott's our best and he's on it!

I've issued a Decommission Order - the MAG PARABELLUM's are GONE!"

"...This is your LAST reprieve, Anderson!

Is that CLEAR!"

Shouting - Macabe's eyes are glowing.

"Yes Sir, VERY CLEAR!" Anderson sweats.

Macabe's face instantly disappears off the screen, as General Anderson takes a deep breath and blankly stares back at the blacked-out monitor screen.

Chapter 4

MAG PARABELLUM

NEAR FONTANA DAM - CHEROKEE MORGUE - QUALLA BOUNDARY

As we visually enter the Morgue hallway of the CHEROKEE POLICE Department, the distinct sound of CLICKING from the soles of snake skin boots, walking and striking tiles can be heard.

Chief Vann points to a heavy doorway and makes his way down a silent corridor toward it, with the two SBI Officers at his six, trying to catch up.

Vann reaches into his leather coat pocket and removes some LATEX GLOVES, then grabs a SURGICAL MASK from a box at the doorway entrance, as he places it over his nose and mouth gesturing for the Agents to do the same.

At once, they enter the Morgue Viewing room together.

Chief Vann steps up to a bald NATIVE AMERICAN man, Coroner Bull, wearing heavy coke bottle glasses as he intensely focuses on a CORPSE, the same decomposed body from the dam incident. He's working on it.

Near the cadaver drawers at the back of the room, another man, Lab-Man, dressed identically in a waterproof surgical gown stares at the motley crew as it enters. The Chief speaks first.

"Morning, Doc."

"Same to you Chief, but this is wa'aay too early for autopsy results."

"Didn't expect it, Bull. . .

These Guys have a Warrant for some objects and fragments."

"Like what? BULLETS!" Bull spits out.

"I'll need those to write up my report, if I find any, Chief!"

"Just dig 'em out, Bull, Now!

And have Lab-Man take a few pictures for the records."

Lab-Man quickly takes his cue and rushes up to the CORPSE, camera in hand, then waits in position like an obedient puppy, for the DOC to start his cut.

"Okay then, but I'm on record, that this is not our protocol, Chief."

"It's on me, Bull, Just do it!" The Chief shouts at him.

Bull, starts working, digging, feeling, and moving organs with incredible agility. . .THEN he finds a fragment, then another, then another as they clink onto a nearby stainless surgical tray, with Bull looking them over one by one, then he releases them.

One FRAG falls to the floor near the shoes of the First SBI Officer, along with a large piece of rotted blackened GUT attached, as both SBI Officers start to retch, then turn toward the sinks on each side of the Lab.

"Hey, got a 'BIG' FYI, Chief,

These fragments are wa'aay too fancy for conventional Bullet Frags.

This stuff smells like high tech Military OPs, if you ask me.

Crazy part though, is this corpse, he's well over seventy years DEAD. Who would of had that kind of advanced technology, way back in those days?"

Chief Vann gets intense as he speaks.

"Shut up and cut 'em out, Doc.

These Guys aren't gonna get any more blood out of us, unless it's paid for!

Warrant or No Warrant!"

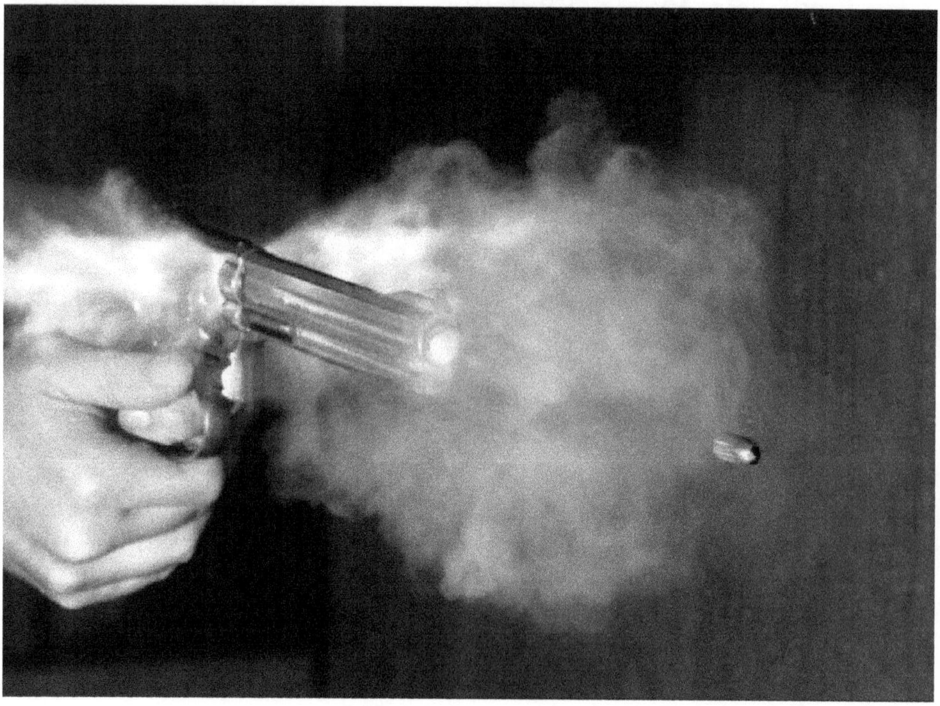

Chapter 5

WKNX TV NEWS

KNOXVILLE, TN - BUILDING LOBBY

Blond mid-thirties, it's Trish Freeman. Trish ENTERS through the gold Art Deco rotating doors at the Gay Street main entrance. Her skirt is tantalizingly short, showing off her long slender legs and red Jimmy Choo ankle strap heels as she clicks across the marble, then blows a sexy kiss and wink to the youthful security guard. . . He knows her well.

Without checking, he waves her though to enter the center elevator in the elaborately gilded WPA Deco styled Lobby. She's on her Cell as she ENTERS the elevator; reacting to her Cell phone call with her WKNX Camera Gal Annie, she gets heated.

"Come on. . . He did what?

 You're off the Fontana Corpse Story, Annie?

Somebody higher up than our Producer, told us to cancel the photo shoot . . .

and the interview at the Dam, as well." Trish pauses.

Am I included in this underhanded crap, too?"

"You don't know?"

"Just TEXT me the details, and I'll send over the rest of my video Library file to your TEXT, Annie."

Trish reacts as the doors open on her floor.

"Okay, I got it, Annie.

Gotta go now, I'm at my meeting!"

THE WKNX EXECUTIVE OFFICES

Bill Berman is the WKNX TV NEWS Bureau CHIEF and CEO. He's in his late 50's and has recently been promoted to the Knoxville Division from a major Washington DC based News Network.

He's been waiting for his top female field Anchor all morning, to welcome her on her latest scoop.

Underlying his good-natured smile, he has an ominous concern about a sudden call he got from the FBI.

Trish holding her coffee, enters the room escorted by Berman's secretary Liz. As Liz exits, closing the door. . .

"Thank you, Liz!"

Berman adds, as he puts down his private phone and reverts to his corporate smiling face and soft response.

"Well, well, Ms. Freeman, what a fortuitous event at your remote shoot. . . Congratulations!"

Trish viciously aims her coffee mug at Bill, then takes the seat across facing him, as her smile and voice turn serious angry.

"Where can I put this, BILL?"

(Up your Ass she thinks)

"Anywhere, Trish!" Bill grins back at her.

"Damn it! What the fuck is up now, Bill? Why'd you call me in here this early! You knew I was researching this thing in detail . . .

And I need time to dig out the real story behind it."

"We'll, that's why you're here, Trish." He smiles at her.

"It's all on hold and you're off 'Bird-Dog', for the moment!"

"So WHO got to you, Bill?" She growls. One of those asshole Washington Bigwigs? I saw you slither that phone down, as I came in. This is a serious story that will make my career Bill. . . Don't cut my legs out now."

To be honest with you, Trish, it was the FBI, not our office. But that was my morning call.

The one I just hung up was my long-time go-to friend at the Bureau. Someone that knows how really serious this whole thing is. That's why you're here, Trish!"

Bill turns off his intercom, gets up and LOCKS the office door then returns to a seat beside Trish.

"Oh my GAWD! You are serious, Bill!"

"Trish, just shut up and listen!

The top brass, the 'bigwigs' as you call them, even going back to the 'J Edgar Hoover Days' at the FBI, knew that Roosevelt had given another Agency, even higher authority, priority and power than the FBI.

Hoover always loathed Roosevelt and others for that fact, but he was Domestic Only and powerless to do anything!

This ALSOS Agency was 'Universal', like today's CIA – but on STEROIDS. . . without any constraints or controls by anyone in Government.

They were the ultimate 'Wartime Cowboys'! Secret WWII US and British Operatives and Spies with Presidential and Prime Minister 'Carte Blanche'.

They had an unlimited budget, they could do anything to anyone. NO oversight by Our Congress nor British Parliament and a mission to recover, detain indefinitely, or **'assassinate'** anyone that threatened the Manhattan Project. It was an "Octopus" of Power and Abuse, Trish!"

"Oh Fuck, Bill!" Trish looks scared.

"Are these guys still around today? It's been over seventy years since the Atomic-Bomb Project and World War II! And even the Cold War is over! Why are they still here? Seriously, Bill, how deep does this go, and why are they into 'My Story'?"

Bill doesn't answer. He simply gets up and goes back to his seat behind the desk and unlocks a private drawer, takes out some papers and returns to Trish's side. Then hands Trish the Documents as he speaks.

"Trish, here's the Official statement on ALSOS!

General Leslie Groves, the man 'hand-picked' by President Roosevelt, created ALSOS; and guess what ALSOS means in Greek, **'Groves'**!

Trish intensely looks over the Docs as she reacts.

"Hah! **'Groves'**, That's his name, what an egotistical power monger!

I can't believe this!

More Government bullshit, Bill!"

"It gets deeper, Trish!"

Bill looks even more serious.

"General Leslie R. Groves created the Manhattan Project and 'handpicked' Oppenheimer to run it. Groves was involved in all aspects of the Atomic Bomb's development: Security, Selection of sites like Oak Ridge, Tennessee; Los Alamos, New Mexico; and Hanford, Washington.

But lastly, this man became the hidden government power behind your Story!

He Held the 'Golden Hand' over the TVA Power Grid allocation for Oak Ridge's Y-12 and K-25 Nuclear Plants and ALCOA's B-17 and B-29 Aircraft Material Production near War's end, by secretly rushing to complete Fontana Dam's massive electric power project from 1942, in less than three years. He even had a hand in arranging 'Operation Paperclip' to recruit NAZI Scientists into the US after the War."

Suddenly, a red light began blinking persistently on Bill's phone, then another, then another. He glances toward it, then turns back to Trish. Her eyes watering with intensity and emotion, Trish reacts.

"So, what happened to ALSOS? Groves is dead, by now. Why is all this still going on behind the scenes?"

Bill realized he was out of time.

"Once, the Hiroshima and Nagasaki A-Bomb Blasts took place, ALSOS had developed over 200 Operatives both American and British, but officially the Executive Office of the President disbanded it on October 15th, 1945.

Yet, in reality, since Roosevelt was dead, Truman was never informed of its existence, so he actually never signed that Executive Order to Disband it."

"Oh my GAWD, Bill!

And Groves never disbanded it either! It's still alive?"

Bill's eyes give her the answer she was asking for.

He then jumps up and rushes to his desk phone, hitting Liz's line first.

"Liz, sorry.

Just hold them ALL for a couple more minutes, thanks!"

He turns back to Trish with a very ominous look on his face.

"Trish, you can't let this out. Not a word, 'til we get more facts. But if you find anything, run it by me first.

Off the Record, you are free to pursue all angles. You must be careful though, we don't know who's running this, who's watching us or what they might decide to do."

"Damn! It sounds dangerous, Bill. But that's just the kind of Story, I love!

Excitement or Sex! GAWD, I Love 'em both, Bill!"

Bill watches her eyes intently. Her enthusiasm has taken over as she exudes her power. She's young, energetic, very sexy and lastly, Naive. He knows he'll have to keep an eye on her.

In an unexpected move, Trish looks down at the Document one last time, then hands it back to Bill. As he fumbles with it, she quickly undoes the top two buttons of her blouse, exposing her beautiful tanned skin and the deep cleavage between her breasts.

"You know what?

It's hot as Hell in here, Bill!

And time for me to get out, and back up the road to Fontana!"

Suddenly she gets up then goes to the door, turning to him with a sexy twinkle in her eyes, as she shakes her hair askew, and unlocks it.

"Liz probably thinks I've been fucking your eye balls out! Or maybe, sucking them out, Ha! But we'll deal with that cronyism tale some other time, won't we Bill!"

In Bill's mind, that sounded like an incredible idea, as he silently moves back behind his desk, grinning as she leaves.

Trish again LAUGHS, as the door opens and Liz stands facing her, with a knowing smile on HER FACE, too.

Chapter 6

THE CHEROKEE NATION CASINO

THE WESTERN SMOKEY MOUNATINS - PANORAMIC

We fly in, high over the Great Smoky Mountains above the Cherokee Indian Reservation, over one hundred miles EAST of KNOXVILLE, then look downward into the town of CHEROKEE, North Carolina. . . FOCUS is on a small river running beside a massive CASINO RESORT. . .

But, you can't see THE MAN's face as he heads into the massive CHEROKEE CASINO & RESORT LOBBY. It's mid-afternoon and still hot outside as a refreshing cool air breeze flushes in all around the interior. The clanging sound of slot machines and winner bells fills the entire entrance.

THE MAN crosses the Lobby without attention and quickly enters one of three Elevators. Within moments he's exiting the large elevator in an upper floor hallway as all at once

THE MAN's face comes into FULL VIEW - we're looking at Jack Wolcott.

Using a handheld techno device, Wolcott quickly disarms the security KEY to ROOM 5575 and slides unnoticed into the Room, as the alarm system -- beep...beep -- ends abruptly.

Once inside, Jack scans the room and without displacing anything, mentally indexes its contents and prepares his welcoming gear. He checks the target suitcases and sets a backup device inside each of them, just in case.

Finally, in the closet, he sets up his controls, calls in, then positions himself for the arrival of his prey.

THE POLICE OFFICES AT CHEROKEE, NC

In another part of the small Cherokee town, the two SBI OFFICERS drive out of the Qualla Morgue Parking Lot with a black box filled with Bullet Fragments from the still unidentified FONTANA CORPSE.

Entering the Interstate ramp, they speed directly over to the CHEROKEE CASINO & RESORT less than five miles away to collect their gear from their overnight room.

The First SBI Officer is the driver -- The Second SBI Officer is checking the black box and recording his comments on an audio tape device, as a call comes in from their SBI BOSS in RALEIGH on the car phone. Its quickly shifted to the car's speaker phone as . . . the BOSS speaks:

"Give me a Status update!"

The FIRST SBI OFFICER switches to his ear phone and states.

"We've executed the Warrant and have the Fragments. Should be at the Raleigh Office by 1800, Boss!"

The SBI BOSS says something back that's indistinguishable to us in earphone as he replies. . .

"Roger Boss, see you there! Out!"

The SECOND SBI OFFICER then asks,

"What'd he say?"

"He said, Be Alert. Others are aware of this evidence we're transporting and may want this whole damn thing shut down."

Instantly, the SECOND SBI OFFICER grabs a GLOCK from under his seat and checks its magazine load, then slams an extra clip into his belt.

"It's probably nothing, but we can't be too careful."

In minutes, they arrive at the massive CHEROKEE CASINO & RESORT LOBBY and head directly to ROOM 5575.

As they enter the ROOM, the telephone STARTS RINGING - loud and insistent.

The two SBI Officers split and The First SBI Officer goes for the phone, the Second SBI Officer moves to grab their suitcases; both are completely focused - occupied with distractions

AS

Jack Wolcott scanning out of the closet MOVES ON THEM - everything happens fast - FIRST SBI OFFICER

(pointing with the phone)

"Behind you!"

"What?" The SECOND SBI OFFICER surprised.

Both hesitate - just a moment - Bad Decision

SLAM! - out of nowhere - Jack is holding a massive syringe with a killer needle, as he quickly injects fluid into the neck of the Second SBI Officer.

Instantly, that takes out the critical target with the GUN.

-- But THE GUN IS KNOCKED OUT OF HIS UNFASTENED HOLSTER

And SLIDES into the bathroom across the floor tiles --

The other SBI Officer is in motion toward Jack - backhanding him off balance and - rushing into the bathroom.

This is war - as Jack jumps back in to cut him off. It's a flat-out, close-quarters death struggle. . .

BUT

Jack still hammered from that powerful opening backhand - drives the remaining Officer's head back, as they both struggle for The GUN . . . BLAMM!!! - wild shot - into the shower -

But that NOISE, Jack DID NOT WANT.

Now in play on the UPPER FLOOR HALLWAY - a Maid working the floor HEARS the GUN's discharge and knows immediately.

Instinctively, she runs to the Elevator and hits the FIRE ALARM.

With a WIDE VIEW OF THE UPPER HALLWAY and the CLARION SOUND DEAFENING, several room doors instantly open with dazed guests heading to the Elevator - but its DOORS are frozen open. '

USE THE STAIRS' is flashing everywhere. The pandemonium is perfect, it's the distraction and protection Jack Wolcott needs.

The BATHROOM scene in ROOM 5575 has them both still wrestling - as Jack slams the Officer's face and breaks his nose, then kicks the GUN out of his hand.

AT last, arms locked around the Officer's throat - UNTIL

- it's done and the BODY slumps against the tub.

Now Jack's ultra ALSOS skills kick in, as he rushes out of the bathroom to locate the FRAGMENT Case, but it's NOT THERE

. . Must be back in the State Vehicle. Their SBI Sedan.

Frenzied, Jack performs a fast professional CLEAN, BODY staging and all . . . then removes all his gear, grabs the Sedan's Keys and conveniently disappears as ordained by LUCK, into the mass Chaos outside the CASINO RESORT.

FINALLY, INSIDE THE STATE SBI SEDAN, Jack immediately secures the bullet fragment case and checks its contents to complete this part of his mission.

The CASINO CLARION ALARM and the arriving FIRE and POLICE SIRENS fill the background, as Jack quickly exfils past the emergency caravans, then drives the State SBI Sedan Westward onto the Interstate ramp to begin his next assignment -

Tennessee. . .

Chapter 7

THE WKNX NEWS ANCHOR

OUT OF THE WESTERN SMOKIES TO KNOXVILLE

ALSOS OPERATIONS - WASHINGTON DC

Four of the OPERATIVES from the first ALSOS CONFERENCE ROOM SCENE plus several women operators are in motion at the BULLPEN - behind arrays of CIA, NSA and NASA Computer and Satellite Monitoring Systems.

The place is cranking - cells to COULEE ALSOS HQ - lines to forward AGENTS and SECONDARY FIELD CONTACTS and lastly a News contact somewhere near Knoxville, Tennessee

Within the ALSOS BULLPEN General Anderson is watching in the background - Blanc and Rita at their work stations -

While Yuan, code name MONARCH - the General's aide de camp, on mobile, turns to Anderson as he begins speaking into a speaker phone. . .

"This is MONARCH - Your clean-up status?"

Jack responds back.

"Both targets IMMOBILE but not NEUTRALIZED - THE PACKAGE is in-hand and the target's vehicle is BURNED"

Yuan looks at Anderson.

"Are you ready for your next mission?"

Jack quizzes back,

"In transit now - ten minutes out - but I need the GPS coordinates and which plan of attack?"

Across the room -- RITA reacts, as the General points Yuan's eyes toward her workstation - then 'cut motions' Yuan to mute the CALL.

Anderson speaks . . .

"Where IS that Reporter Bitch, Rita?"

Rita working fast - Computer keys and her robotic GUI moves with her eyes, and without looking up -

"SHE's just leaving the News Building's Parking Garage and is headed EAST/SOUTHEAST to Maryville, Tennessee - Twenty-Eight minutes out."

Oh, and Destinations on her NAV show FONTANA - then the QUALLA MORGUE.

SHE's alone! NSA CELL-SENSOR's indicate she appears aggressive and emotional, but her BMW will need GAS in thirty minutes."

Anderson looks back at MONARCH.

"Okay, Yuan, we need to know how much she knows, - who she touches and where she goes, before we move to our next TARGET."

Anderson adds,

"Tell him it's a HONEYTRAP MISSION. . .

Follow her 'til it needs to end, then Accident Style TERMINATION!"

Anderson then motions Yuan to un-mute the CALL

"This is MONARCH, back again!

Your Mission, HONEYTRAP - INFO then A-TERMINATE

I repeat, HONEYTRAP - INFO then A-TERMINATE!"

Driving Hard, we find a LARGE BLACK MURDERED-OUT CHEVY SUBURBAN, then focus on Jack Wolcott's eyes - no emotion - as his hands on the wheel in the SUV Interior - He's quickly passing Interstate Signs, Bridges, Cars, Eighteen Wheelers - He's a driven machine operating on pure instinct, no feelings as he comments on speaker phone. . .

"ACKNOWLEDGED! - HONEYTRAP - INFO, then A-TERMINATE"

Inside ALSOS OPERATIONS - WASHINGTON DC

Yuan reacts back almost robotic-like.

"We are uploading NOW - Details to your NAV and Computer -

OUT!"

Wolcott checks his NAV screen as in floods a mass of GPS and STATUS information on Trish Freeman, including photos, personal details, the works.

The competed transmission, 'disappears' Jack Wolcott's call off MONARCH'S screen

THEN -

Inside ALSOS OPERATIONS, Blanc suddenly gets excited about his ON-SCREEN MONITOR -

"Hey! They've got both SBI Officers Out Alive from the CASINO RESORT!"

New data feeds instantly across several INFO monitor screens - Everyone in the BULLPIN rushes to look.

Electrified energy, except - Anderson whose 'bullhorn voice' hits everyone.

"Back to WORK - that was the PLAN, Folks"

Anderson then turns to Yuan.

"What's up with that Indian Chief we've been monitoring?"

Yuan reacts, pointing to Blanc's Monitor. . .

"He's there, too"

Quickly, Anderson FOCUSES on Blanc's Monitor as Yuan continues.

"Along with several other Officers and the QUALLA Tribal Chief." Yuan pauses.

"Should I Monitor them too?"

Anderson yells back,

"NO! Just put your priority NSA FOCUS SYSTEM on that CHIEF OF POLICE, we need to know, what he knows. . .

cause He's our next trouble maker. . . without a doubt!"

EXTERIOR OF A SHELL STATION AND C-STORE - MARYVILLE, TN

Rain is beginning to hit the windshield of Trish Freeman's 5-SERIES BMW SEDAN as she slows to enter the Pump Bay carefully, aligning her right rear side gas door with the High Octane Pump.

She jumps out quickly to insert her Credit Card and start the pump, then runs inside the C-Store to get an energy bar - a chilled STARBUCKS carry-out coffee - and check her TEXT messages,

JUST AS

Jack Wolcott drives into the same Station area just beside her BMW at parallel gas pumps. . .

Quickly, he CODES-OUT her vacant car's electrical system with his NSA OVERRIDE DEVICE then lastly, CONVERTS his BLACK MURDERED-OUT CHEVY SUBURBAN into a Private Limo, places a TOURZ App sign in his right dash screen, and waits, as the rain STOPS.

Seemingly unnoticed a MAN enters the Shell C-STORE and picks up a few items. He's at the register just a slight moment before Trish.

To distract her, Jack EYES a CAMARO Cap and Cell phone behind the counter, as he addresses the Clerk. . .

"Hey DUDE, you a MUSTANG or CAMARO GUY?"

The Clerk smiles, happy he asked.

"CHEVY CAMARO 275HP, MAN, all the way!"

Jack cajoles him,

"DAMN DUDE, ME TOO! Love those RODS!

Tell you what - Let me have about Five Dollars, NO, NO . . . make it Twenty-Five on those 100K QUIK-PIC LOTTO Tickets. (then he glances back behind, at Trish, to make sure she's good and irritated)

"You know, Today's my 'LUCK DAY' and I'm go'in up to that INDIAN CASINO to WIN at those BLACKJACK and CRAPS Tables, while I'm HOT!"

Jack continues to drag it out, as he casually banters with the CLERK about his work and the HARRAH'S CHEROKEE CASINO - purposely wasting time to get Trish really steamed.

She's right behind almost pushing his backside, along with at least five others, also annoyed, as she 'coughs out a response', with eyes on fire, (she needs to get moving). . .

"If you don't Get On The 'MOVE MISTER', your Luck's gonna hit Rock- Bottom, and your Dice are gonna get 'ICE' Cold!"

Jack reacts smoothly . . .

"UT-Oh . . . Sorry, LADY. . . Real Sorry! (glances at Trish, then the Dude) Check me out, Dude! And keep the change, 'cause this Lady just might have a 'Pistol Packing' in Her Purse for both of us!"

Trish finally smiles at him . . .

"Hah, Hah, now that's actually funny, MISTER!"

Jack grabs his Lotto Tickets and grins back at her, as he quickly moves out through the doorway and continues toward his SUV smiling.

It's a BUSY STATION - Lots of customers are pulling in and out

AS

Trish finally exits with her coffee and bag of treats, then 'keys' HER BMW - IT won't START!

She tries AGAIN - AGAIN - then AGAIN. NOW, even her BMW's Doors won't OPEN, as she seethes out loud!

"What the Hell??"

She's super irritated now!

"SHIT! . . . SHIT, SHIT, DOUBLE SHIT!

What the Hell is going on with You, BABY?"

Trish looks up and spies that MAN, it's Jack watching her nearby, so she waves to him. He holds his position, just to observe and deepen her MAD frustration

AS

She finally gets up the nerve - starts prancing toward him.

And speaks in a suddenly friendly tone. . .

"Hey MISTER, I know we didn't hit it off too well, in there! But You sounded like a CAR GUY?"

Jack smiles at her.

"You're right, LADY . . . But I forgive you."

Trish frowns, at first, then shrugs it off and really smiles at him.

Jack's got her.

"I am, a CAR GUY, Miss . . . Name's Jack! Jack Anders . . ."

Then grinning at Trish, he adds. . .

"AMERICAN CARS only, though! I'm a DRIVER and sometimes a mechanic, but I 'do' know what's wrong, with your GIRL!"

Trish is desperate. . .

"What do you think then, Mr. Anders?"

Jack pauses for effect.

"Well . . .

A catastrophic failure!

Happens on those GERMAN Beauties All the time."

Jack walks to the BMW and takes out the fueling NOZZLE - replaces the CAP and CLOSES the FUEL DOOR. Then looks around the BMW as Trish stares at him in wonder.

"Looks like a 2014 5-SERIES BMW They'll have to TOW you to a Dealership. . . and without a Warranty your looking at thousands to replace the entire electronics system!"

Now he's got her, as she's about to cry, and pleads sexy to him.

"Oh GAWD, Mr. Anders. . . I haven't got that kind of "Time or Money". I've got a serious Appointment at FONTANA DAM with a KEY MANAGER and another one in CHEROKEE, not far from THE CASINO and RESORT, where I overheard, you're going."

She uses a long pause for drama, eyes on Jack.

"Mr. Anders, You're a Driver, Right? Could you take me, there? I'll make it worth your while. My TV STATION will cover your expenses! Please. . ."

Jack has a serious shock on his face, damn she's sexy.

"First, Miss, I'm actually Off Duty. **a TOURZ** Driver. There's an APP on your Cell Phone for **TOURZ.** . ."

Jack takes a serious pause. . .

"May I ask your name, Miss?"

Trish stalls a moment, while she quickly checks her phone SEARCH - sure nuff, she sees **TOURZ** Apps on-line and Jack Anders - a DRIVER as well.

Trish is embarrassed, but hopeful as . . .

"OKAY, Got it. . . **TOURZ** - That's Fantastic!

OH - I'm so, so Sorry, Jack! My name's Trish Freeman -

I'm the LEAD FIELD REPORTER at **WKNX- TV**. . .

I'm working a major COLD-CASE MURDER up on the Cherokee Nation Reservation, in North Carolina."

Finally, Jack puts on his real friendly grin -

"Well, Trish, YOU actually Had Me at, "Oh GAWD, Mr. Anders"!"

They both begin LAUGHING, as Jack walks back to his SUV - Trish continues watching him, with another pleading look, as she bites her lip, shy and sexy at him.

"Just ONE other request, Jack!"

(long pause to see his reaction)

"I need my Briefcase. . .

And also my Suitcase, from the TRUNK of my car.

But it's LOCKED-UP too. . ."

In a flash Jack opens his SUV and retrieves a small kit, smiling, he returns with a screw driver, as he secretly keys a small device hidden from her view, to override the BMW TRUNK LOCK -

In moments, he grabs both her CASES and heads over to the SUV, just as, unexpectedly, his heart starts pounding, not with FEAR, but CARNAL ENERGY, as the ultra-sexy Trish Freeman runs over to him and plants an unexpected KISS on his CHEEK.

Then, while, as he watches her sexy body movement - she slides slowly into his SUV's passenger side, short shirt, long sexy-legs, red strapped JIMMY CHOOS, smiling coyly at him; and all the time playing with his mind.

Chapter 8

ONWARD TO FONTANA

OUT OF TENNESSEE INTO THE SMOKIES

INSIDE THE LARGE BLACK MURDERED-OUT CHEVY SUBURBAN

We first focus on Jack Wolcott, then to Trish Freeman as after an hour of driving they've gotten familiar with each other as Trish's small talk continues.

Watching the road ahead. Trish finally seems relaxed, even with this strange man she just met.

Jack glances at Trish and smiles. . .

"So, Trish, tell me more about your life in Germany. . ."

Trish seems to drift into her own imaginary world as she begins to finish the story she began earlier in the drive.

"Well, as I said before, Jack, By the time I was twelve, I was tall and lanky. That's the year I realized why, we had been to so many Military Bases all my early life.

My father was in Military Intelligence. He was never home. And my mother was a beautiful blond German Gretchen." (Trish made a soft laugh, as she relaxed into the story)

"She had met Dad in England. . . But she was also away from home often, in Germany, so the Base School provided my care most of the time they were both away." (Trish tensed up as she added)

"Then, I found out they were divorcing.

She had been having an affair with another Officer in Germany. It was real messy, but something happened.

My Dad didn't seem the same. . .

He came home one afternoon about ten years ago and told me she had died in a Car accident on the Autobahn.

That's when I got my urge to investigate things and just before we were transferred back to the States, I found out she was killed in a Military owned Mercedes, with that same Officer she had left Dad for.

It seemed unusual that Dad never mentioned it to me, but he was always a closed book.

So I began to investigate 'him'. That's when my search came to a dead-end.

Jack, he was a Black Ops Agent within his own MI Unit!"

Jack Wolcott NOW glances intense at Trish.

"Did you recover from that, Trish?"

Trish looks back at Jack in despair and again spins deeper into her dream world as she continues her story, with moisture welling up in her eyes.

Suddenly, Trish focuses on Jack's face and smiles almost lovingly.

"Well, I Loved my Dad. More than my mother. Neither were emotionally close to me, but DAD was very protective.

Then, he went to Afghanistan. I was nineteen then.

I had just entered UCLA in Journalism. . .

But, I never saw him again.

My Uncle attended his funeral with me . . .

Full Military Honors, but the casket was closed, so I never knew, if he was really in THERE. . . (now, both her eyes were tearing up)

"Jack, I know you won't believe this, but you look like his younger self . . . An image I can't ever forget from years ago. . .

Maybe that's why, I feel so comfortable around you, Jack?"

Wolcott quickly slows, then pulls the SUV to the roadside.

"You know, Trish. . . You also, remind me of someone in my past life. Someone very precious to me, as well. . .

(Jack pauses, then looks deep into her eyes) And I'll never forget Her, either."

LATER AS THEY DRIVE DEEPER INTO THE MOUNTAINS, AN AERIAL VIEW BEGINS . . .

We see the stark magnificence of the GREAT SMOKY MOUNTAINS in Northwestern North Carolina, many miles East of Maryville, Tennessee.

High above it, we fly into the late Fall Evergreens and Deciduous Trees covering the LITTLE TENNESSEE River Valley, then down along a narrow highway following the River's circuitous path upward to its source.

Below, the rugged sharp rapids of the LITTLE TENNESSEE transformed by thousands of years of weathering, rush behind us downward and West, toward the GREAT TENNESSEE RIVER Valley at the edge of the Mountains near Knoxville.

Climbing higher we enter the narrowest Canyon of the LITTLE TENNESSEE then ascend the ancient concrete walls of CHEOAH DAM, on the RIVER's last high mountain Lake before FONTANA.

At the Lake's end, a narrow flatland holds water birds grazing in the marshes on either side of the River, as they prepare to head away from the coming winter winds.

A little further Eastward and up River, we at last re-enter the narrow Canyon and Highway that ends at the Main Power Station mounted at the base of the massive FONTANA DAM edifice.

LATE THAT AFTERNOON. . .

THEY ARRIVE AT THE POWER STATION AT FONTANA DAM.

A MAN stands inside a RESTRICTED fenced area watching for something -

Around him is a giant POWER GRID of HUMMING Transformers and massive Electrical Gear generating enormous amounts of ENERGY as it passes to Power Lines above him.

The tallest concrete DAM in the Eastern United States stands behind the MAN, as he waits. He's Charley "Red Bird" Johnson, Manager of the TVA FONTANA COMPLEX.

Panning down the entrance road, we can see in the distance a Black SUV. We follow it as it gets closer then STOPS,

AS

Jack turns directly to Trish Freeman, as she prepares to EXIT, with briefcase in hand.

(Jack knows something now and looks intense, but smiles)

"Well, Trish, we're here! Looks like your INTERVIEW is waiting - but where's your CAMERAMAN?"

Trish begins "LAUGHING". . .

(she's ready, set and sexy)

"He'll be here, Jack!"

(She pauses, then looks back down the road)

"I can take it from here. And seriously, thanks for getting the BEEMER Place to pick-up my car, Jack." (She pauses)

"You ARE, gonna wait for me then, Jack!"

"Of course, Trish, just like we agreed - I'll be right here! But no more than an hour, Right!"

Trish grins at him.

"No more than an hour, Jack."

(Turning, she sees the TV VAN coming)

"Here he comes! Don't panic, I'll be back. . ."

In a FLASH, Trish is out of the SUV and walking up to her CAMERAMAN's VAN.

Jack watches them carefully, then spots Charley 'Red Bird' Johnson, the TVA Contact, unlocking the GATE and coming out to GREET them.

Jack stalls, waiting until they are ALL completely inside the Power Station Building before he presses the dashboard and reveals the NAS NAV Console, then switches the NAS NAV system back on.

In moments, they are all inside the BUILDING ENTRANCE and into THE MASSIVE GENERATOR ROOM

Charley Red Bird Johnson's acts as a TOUR GUIDE of small talk, to ease his own nerves. . .

"These THREE GENERATORS can power over 150,000 Homes at capacity and put out 300 Million Watts of Electricity."

Trish VIEWs the room, then back to her CAMERAMAN'S FACE as they together. . .

"WOW, what MASSIVE ENGINEERING!"

All three slowly walk along the upper observation deck, then disappear into Charley Red Bird's OFFICE.

INSIDE THE FONTANA POWER STATION OFFICE

Trish and her Cameraman set up silently in Charley 'Red Bird's' OFFICE -

Trish takes a seat in front of Charley 'Red Bird', with her Cameraman behind and slightly to her right front side - HE's transmitting the VIDEO DATA to the WKNX VAN's RECORDING UNIT -

AND

UNKNOWINGLY - directly into Jack's NAS NAV SYSTEM.

WITHIN JACK'S BLACK MURDERED-OUT SUV -

Jack's EYES are on the NAV SCREEN MONITOR, as he picks up all the ACTION!

On Jack's MONITOR we see Trish and Charley 'Red Bird' Johnson's in the Office LIVE as -

Trish is focused and intense . . .

"Before we get started -

Do you prefer Mr. Johnson or Charley 'Red Bird'?"

Charley is uncomfortable, but willing.

"Either is fine, Ms. Freeman."

Trish glances back at her CAMERAMAN.

"OH, Mr. Red Bird - just call me Trish.

So Let's get Started. . .

Mr. Red Bird, tell me some background on what happened to FONTANA. . . The OLD TOWN and the CHEROKEE INDIAN property on EAGLES CREEK?"

Charley thinking silently, then it flowed out -

"That STORY goes back many, many years before the DAM, Trish. The CHEROKEE NATION has always had things taken from it, if it suits the GOVERNMENT, without PROTEST.

Hundreds of Years back a SACRED Burial GROUND was located on EAGLE CREEK at the LITTLE TENNESSEE River. In the late 1880's that was the actual land, that the ORIGINAL FONTANA Town was on.

LEGEND has it, that massive amounts of GOLD NUGGETS, some as big as baseballs, could be found just lying on the ground out there - But NO ONE in the QUALLA INDIAN NATION would touch them - They were SACRED STONES."

Trish is shocked, then looks at her CAMERAMAN.

"Oh my GAWD, Charley - When, did the outside World find out about this GOLD?"

Charley looks sad and tenses up, concern on his face.

"That would be Mrs. Wood from New York, she came down with the Montvale Lumber Company, About the 1890's.

She's the one who first named the Logging Camp, 'FONTANA'.

She even knew George Vanderbilt personally, when he was in Railroads, so he helped her get the GOVERNMENT Lumber and Timber Rights to our SACRED INDIAN LAND on Eagle Creek.

They said, she spent a great deal of time around there, ALONE at first. Some think she even hired renegade CHEROKEE'S to find the surface GOLD, and paid them well for each one they found.

By 1907 she moved the Tent Encampment to the top of the creek where they had found COPPER.

That's when they built the permanent town of FONTANA.

This was no tent town. It was a Village of nicely built houses, a community store, a school building, a medical building, a church, the Fontana Hotel and even a US Post Office. Why even a standard gauge railroad was soon built by Vanderbilt's Railroad to haul goods back and forth to Asheville and out EAST.

But our QUALLA INDIAN NATION got none of it, LAND or GOLD -

We were simply pushed out and our SACRED BURIAL GROUNDS gone!

Trish again reacts shocked at his story, and its vicious 'Revelations'.

"So what happened to the GOLD, Charley?"

She becomes strongly insistent. . .

"Who took the GOLD out. . . And WHY do you think that has anything to do with this MURDER. . .

or ALLEGED MURDER, since the CORONER'S findings on the CORPSE that blasted out of the DAM'S SLUICE GATES last week, are still inconclusive."

Inside the SUV, the we FOCUS on Jack, then see the MONITOR with Trish Freeman steamed, as SHE waits for Charley Red Bird Johnson's answer. . .

Jack now has MONARCH on his internal speaker phone watching Trish struggle uncomfortably - She herself begins to realize how deep this SHIT goes.

AS

Yuan to Jack's transmission on speaker phone, reacts pissed. . .

"This is quickly getting OUT OF CONTROL, Jack!

Jack stands his ground, urgently insistent. . .

"Look Yuan, you now have the PACKAGE. All of these TARGETS down here can be IMMOBILE or NEUTRALIZED once we know what they've found out." Jack pauses.

"I have it all UNDER CONTROL. . . Just give me TIME to ID all the PLAYERS,

We'll MOVE on them, Like Lightning - Then, I'll CLEAN IT UP!"

SUDDENLY WE'RE BACK TO THE OFFICE SCENE LIVE

Trish's Cameraman moves in CLOSER and PANS from Trish's face to Charley 'Red Bird' Johnson's

AS

They WAIT for Charley's Answer!

Charley looks mentally exhausted. . .

"I'm running out of time, Ms. Freeman. Maybe we should finish this up after the CORONER'S INQUEST is complete."

Trish again, strongly insistent. . .

"Charley, Please, can we just get your take on all the GOLD that was there in the now flooded town of FONTANA back in '41, just when this DAM was being built?

How does it connect to this ALLEGED MURDER?"

She raised his blood pressure, with that one!

Now, he's really uptight, as he reacts loudly.

"I'M DONE!

Maybe you should talk to Chief Vann at the QUALLA POLICE OFFICE in CHEROKEE.

One of his MEN had family living down on EAGLE CREEK, in the time before they flooded the VALLEY.

That's all I've got." He clears his throat.

"Good Day, Ms. Freeman!"

Charley gets up, then Trish gets up too and waves her Cameraman to CUT the SESSION –

"PACK-UP"

Trish comes back sincere, and somewhat apologetic.

"Charley, Thank You."

Quickly they all begin to walk out - AS - Trish Adds

"And Charley, Thanks for the suggestion to follow-up with Chief Vann."

Jack QUICKLY SHUTS DOWN the NSA NAV SCREEN MONITOR, as he re-aligns the SUV back, to the TOURZ transport vehicle mode, then waits for Trish to wake him from his faked nap.

OUTSIDE THE POWER STATION AT FONTANA DAM

Charley Red Bird Johnson ESCORTS Trish and Her Cameraman through the locked GATE and out to the parking lot,

Then, he waves GOODBYE and quickly returns inside the BUILDING -

Trish WALKS her Cameraman to his VAN and makes some INDISTINGUISHABLE COMMENTS, then heads back to Jack's SUV while waving to the Cameramen as he DRIVES OFF (apparently back to the WKNX-TV STUDIOs in KNOXVILLE).

In moments, she begins TAPPING on the right-side SUV Window and tries to peer through the Black-Out screen, excited to see Jack.

"Jack, are you okay?

I'm ready to go now. Sorry it took so long. Jack, Wake Up!"

Jack finally OPENS her door, rubbing his EYES looking at her beautiful innocent blue eyes, as Trish puts a really sexy smile on him.

"Okay, Sleepy head, Let's go! Now, we can play your LUCKY TABLES!"

Then she gazes at him and adds. . .

"Oh, and get that MARGARITA, you promised me!"

Trish sensually SLIDES into the SUV, LAUGHING at his disheveled look - then PULLS the Door closed, as the SUV disappears back down the same road it came in on.

Chapter 9

CHEROKEE NC

CHEROKEE, NC - HIDDEN DEEP IN THE SMOKIES

HALLWAY, CHEROKEE POLICE BUILDING

Chief Vann walks down the corridor with Andrew Black Hawk, a big hulking Native American Indian with biceps the size of cantaloupes.

"Those SBI Officers were completely BLINDSIDED!"

Black Hawk growls back at him.

"What'd you mean Chief? Turns towards the Chief.

"What I mean is . . . They never saw that coming. And whatever he or she INJECTED 'em with, ERASED their short term memories!"

Black Hawk again growls back.

"This is some HIGH TECH SHIT!

So what's it all mean, to us 'Indians' here in the mountains, Chief?"

"Means WE gotta have a Plan . . . A serious Plan to get this under control and watch our own evidence Close. Put it "Under Guard, Maybe", Hawk."

"Where'd they take 'em? Those Officers, I mean, Chief."

"Down EAST, back to a Hospital in Raleigh. They're out of it, Hawk.

It's our problem, now!"

THEY ENTER CHIEF VANN'S OFFICE:

It's a cramped and sparsely furnished room. The walls are empty of awards, photographs or diplomas, except for a framed image engraving of the Great CHEROKEE INDIAN BRAVE, TSALI. . .

There's very little else to add credibility to the CHIEF's image

AS

Chief Vann pushes into the room ahead of Andrew Black Hawk and EYES suspiciously the two uninvited guests.

Its Coroner Bull, already seated next to another huge NATIVE AMERICAN male - HEAD COUNCIL CHIEF Yona (yho nah) - The Bear!

Coroner Bull is holding a MEDICAL EXAMINERS DOCUMENT tightly

Vann stares an 'arrow' hard at Bull

"I see you've brought THE COUNCIL with you, Doc!"

Then Vann turns to CHIEF Yona with an ugly grin.

"There's nothing for the COUNCIL here, CHIEF Yona, not yet!

We've got other problems to deal with and need to get to the bottom of this, without interference, THEN can we bury HIM."

COUNCIL CHIEF Yona spews an equally vicious stare at Vann.

"You've brought this MATTER to us yourself, Vann . . .

With that unbelievable CASINO INCIDENT!"

The disrespect is thick in the room as CHIEF Yona adds.

"This is going to IMPACT our image and eventually real financial PROFITS to the Nation because of your sloppy and wild eyed ACTIONS. This MATTER should belong to the FEDS, not US!" He then spits out his real reason for being there.

"We need to BURY our OWN, now!

And get this dirty FEDERAL MESS out of our TRIBAL Jurisdiction!"

Chief Vann turns to the front wall, looks at Tsali's image.

"Tsali would NEVER give up on a CHEROKEE DEATH, much less a MURDER by a WHITE MAN." Vann spits back at Yona.

"YOU are weakened by the WHITE'S MONEY, Chief Yona!

YOU, AND the COUNCIL are CORRUPTED,

By all that CASINO PAYOLA!"

Council Chief Yona abruptly stands, with a vicious scowl on his face. Then Coroner Bull rises slowly to join him.

They both start to EXIT Vann's Office,

AS

Chief Vann raises his hand in Coroner Bull's face.

"You're not getting off that easy, Doc . . .

I need that evidence WORKSHEET and your personal opinion, before you leave here.

Coroner Bull reacts, pissed, as he faces Vann.

"Here's the MEDICAL REPORT! Read it for yourself, Chief, then we'll talk!

Council Chief Yona stomps toward the doorway, HE'S REALLY SHOCKED, A FACE that says REVENGE - HE GLARES back at Vann, Then, he grabs the door to shut it and he's GONE.

AS

Coroner Bull hesitates, looking back into Chief Vann's hard stare.

"Don't MOVE, Doc . . ."

Coroner Bull then reacts, to relieve the ROOM's tension.

"Okay, Okay, there's SOLID PROOF, the CORPSE was in fact SHAMAN Wa Ya (why' yah). With the STATE LAB'S DNA and remnants of a CHEROKEE WOLF TATOO hidden in his right shoulder flesh.

Plus, we even analyzed that old TATOO. TRIBAL birch ashes were imbedded in the blackened surface tissue.

In my REPORT, I stated that he was probably MURDERED, then buried in a protected area, probably in a house FLOODED by the DAM way back in '45. Likely somewhere near the EAGLE CREEK section, since that's nearby where he lived."

Now suddenly, Officer Andrew Black Hawk enters the fray for the first time. He's shocked, but fired up!

"Damn, Doc!

That's my 'Great, Great' Uncle. They called him THE WOLF,

The only member of the whole TRIBE, back then, to hold an ENGINEERING DEGREE from the University over in KNOXVILLE.

He was a Civil Mining Engineer and we've still got GOLD and COPPER NUGGET samples, from down on EAGLE CREEK, given by him to THE INDIAN SCHOOL."

Coroner Bull then sadly looks at Officer Black Hawk.

"Well, Andrew, that CORPSE is Wa Ya."

Coroner Bull hands Vann all the papers.

"Here's the FULL REPORT, Chief. But I've got to go."

Vann is now really frustrated, without a come-back.

"Okay, Doc . . . Just get outta here then!"

Coroner Bull, takes a last sullen look at Vann.

"Oh, just one other NOTE, Chief. We detected some unknown POISON in the internal tissues near those FRAGMENTS we extracted from Shaman Wa Ya."

Chief Vann and Andrew Black Hawk suddenly stare back in shock at Bull, their faces say it all.

Chapter 10

CRAPS TABLE TIME

CHEROKEE, NC - THE CASINO - DEEP IN THE SMOKIES

CASINO CRAPS TABLE

We VIEW the massive CASINO Floor, then FOCUS ON Trish and Jack, first they work the Dollar Slots, then Trish rushes over to him, just as her machine goes off LOUDLY, spitting out hundreds in SILVER DOLLAR COINS.

She's SQUEALING for joy, as she kisses his cheek, then rushes back to collect her winnings.

Jack has hit a dry streak and motions a cocktail waitress over to get him more drinks, as he watches Trish.

A Floor Cashier exchanges her winnings for two one-thousand dollar chips, as she returns to Jack, ready to PLAY anything and everything, starting at the CRAPS table.

Drunk on winning and in blind excitement, she yells!

"Come on, Jack, let's go for the GOLD!"

Jack is feeling the effects of several drinks

AS

"Okay, but MY luck's gone cold, You're, gonna role those dice, Trish!"

Briskly they walk into the TABLES area and Trish watches some local High Rollers Crap-Out, at a busy table in the center of the complex.

Trish announces that she wants the DICE and the PLAYERS seeing a BEAUTY with hot legs, all nod in her direction. The DEALER, Mike, surveys the new players and the table players, as they arrive.

The First High Roller watches intensely, as Trish glides up to the Table.

"Go for it, Lady!"

A Second High Roller then adds to the Dealer.

"MIKE, give this 'Lucky' Lady the DICE!"

The DEALER reaches out with the craps stick pushing the DICE towards Trish. She grabs them, as she looks over the regular players around the TABLE, then back to Jack

AS

She kisses him smack on the lips this time . . .

Then smoothly places her one-thousand Dollar CHIP BET on the EIGHT, while Jack is still recovering in shock.

A Regular Player watches her, then commands to the DEALER,

"Let me have five-hundred on hard EIGHT"

The Dealer covers it as the Player responds,

"Thank you, Mike."

Another Player then pushes his CHIPS to the Dealer.

"Give me one-hundred on hard EIGHT, too, Mike!"

As the Dealer reacts, that Player adds,

"Thanks for that, Mike."

Trish takes one last look back at now 'smiling' Jack,

THEN

Trish shakes the Dice with a kiss and ROLLS . . .

"It's a WINNER!" . . . In unison, All the TABLE PLAYERS YELL and CLAP for her, while the HIGH ROLLERS, now hearing the commotion come back to the Table to watch her, for her next move,

AS

Trish places her BETS, then the others follow, including both the High Rollers this time –

AGAIN, it's a WINNER as Trish tosses chips to the Dealer and the PLAYERS toss chips to Trish

The First High Roller watches her shake the DICE,

"You hit it again, 'Lucky Lady', and I'll tip you myself,

One-Thousand dollars!"

The Second High Roller then remarks,

"I'll second that, Lady!"

Trish is now completely excited out of control.

"Okay, Jack, you heard that!"

Jack's busy, as he grabs a CHIP RACK and loads in her TIPS and WINNINGS, it's close to seven-thousand dollars. He places the RACK next to her

AS

Trish SMILES around the Table, titillating the Players,

Then to get Jack's FULL ATTENTION, she LAUGHS OUT to All of them, then the Dealer.

"It's my 'Birthday Number', GUYS!

HARD SIX. . . ALL IN, Mike!"

Jack almost CHOKES, when she again LAUGHS, then ROLLS the DICE

AS

They both SLAM the backboard, first a 'ONE' DIE ROLLS OVER - the TABLE gasps, then the second almost automatic, FLOPS over to a 'FIVE' DIE!

The CROWD building around the TABLE and the Players ALL YELL AGAIN in unison,

"Another Winner!"

As Trish just looks back at Jack and GRINS . . .

"It's your LUCKY DAY, Jack!

And THANK YOU too, Mike!"

Mike's CRAPS STICK sweeps the TABLE as . . .

"Very nice, Mam!

GENTLEMEN and LADIES, Place your bets!"

Both High Rollers, SLIDE ONE-THOUSAND DOLLAR PUMPKINS to Trish, as some of the other Winners throw in several, ONE- HUNDRED DOLLAR CHIPS to tip her performance, as well.

Trish tips the Dealer well, then WAVES and SAYS a sexy "toodle-loo", to the CROWD and the GAMBLERS, as Jack turns to Trish while carrying her incredible WINNINGS TRAY over to the CASINO CASHIER.

"How 'bout our CELEBRATION DRINK, Trish!"

Trish with a sexy grin reacts back to Jack. . .

"And DANCING, too. I'm ready to 'PAR-TAY' tonight, Jack!"

Chapter 11

THE CLUB

THE CHEROKEE CASINO NIGHTCLUB

A dark, seductive atmosphere - there's an intimate crowd of people dancing and drinking, but no one is paying attention.

SOFT JAZZ MUSIC is playing in the background and several couples are romantically embraced in intimate booths lining the room. Several sexy cocktail waitresses are working drinks to the guests on the floor and in the booths.

Jack is ORDERING DRINKS at the BAR.

Before he returns, Trish slides her black 'Victoria Secrets' bra out of her blouse sleeve, then stuffs it into the WINNINGS BAG beside her in the booth.

AS

Jack returns to their booth, with two exotic drinks in hand. He watches her eyes, but she's watching

A COUPLE behind him.

He STOPS and turns around to see them.

A beautiful young Native American girl dancing with a gorgeous woman, maybe 40's, a BLOND wearing a very short skirt, beautiful long legs and spaghetti strap top.

She seductively tosses her long hair, then focuses on Jack. He watches her, TOO LONG. Trish laughs, as Jack quickly turns back to the booth, now noticing for the first time, Trish's hardened nipples pushing out against her silk blouse.

He sets the drinks down and moves in beside her.

Trish again, looks back at the COUPLE, as they finish their routine then SLIDE through the nearby cozy dancing bodies, toward the women's room.

Trish smiles at Jack. . .

"A Toast"

Then Trish sips her drink and remarks to him in a soft sexy voice.

"Did you enjoy that view, Jack?" She pauses to see his reaction.

"I think that Blond likes you. If you want her, I'm sure I can get that arranged for the night."

Stunned at her remark, Jack clears his throat -

"I did enjoy watching her, Trish, but there's someone else I'd rather spend the night with."

Taking a longer than usual sip from her drink, Trish gives him a carnal stare as she pressures her hand down obviously hard, onto his crotch,

"I'll be back shortly, Jack . . .

Your 'HARD-ON' will miss me!"

Then sensually, she slides out of the booth, heading off into the crowd, toward the doorway the COUPLE just entered.

INSIDE THE CLUB'S WOMEN'S ROOM

Dark designer tiles fill the walls and floor, as soft lighting casts shadows into the hallway up to the Hollywood styled make-up area.

CLOSE UP, we see two women are adding lipstick in the mirrors, as the DANCE COUPLE glides into a LARGE EMPTY toilet stall, together.

In moments, Trish enters, clicking in across the tiles with her red Jimmy Choos, then pushes with abandon through their unlocked stall door -

Trish looks excited, as she watches the young Native American girl. It's Doe Angel and she's sucking on a perfectly rolled joint, being lit by The Blond.

Then, without even acknowledging Trish's intrusion, The Blond pulls down Doe Angel's top and begins suckling her right nipple, enthralling Trish's eyes with her exotic expression.

Doe Angel's stoned but sexy voice echoes in the stall. . .

"What can we do for you, Pretty?

(As Doe takes another hit)

"Would you like some too?"

Without answering, Trish takes a big suck off Doe Angel's joint, then savors it, exhaling upward.

Trish's now strained voice from the 'HIT', still sounds sexy

AS

"My friend needs some serious company tonight.

And you two BEAUTIES are perfect."

Doe Angel more stoned than ever and very aroused.

"And what about you, Pretty?"

Then Doe begins urging to the Blond. . .

"HARDER, Baby, HARDER!"

The Blond then looks back to Trish. . .

"He looks really big, Pretty. . . Maybe you should taste him first, yourself."

Watching the Blond work her hand deep into Doe's panties, Trish accepts another drag off Doe Angel's withering joint, this time exhaling downward to the Blond as Doe Angel sides her hand up and into Trish's braless Blouse, arousing her reddened nipples even harder.

Trish's now totally stoned voice, reveals. . .

"Don't want him to know, how bad, I really want him. But, I'd LOVE to WATCH you two, with him first!

And you BEAUTIES, SOOOH turn me on."

The Blond catches on right away, as her deep and stoned voice asks for the plan?

"How do we PLAY IT, then, Pretty?"

Trish's voice becomes urgent. . .

"It's Trish, you can call me Trish."

The Blond smoothly knowing what she wants. . .

"Okay, it's Trish, then!

I'm GABBY and this is DOE.

Trish pulls out a 'High Rollers' Hotel room key.

"Here's my ROOM KEY.

I haven't gone up there yet, but it's BIG, a BIG SUITE.

When you get there, ORDER some HIGH PRICED CHAMPAGNE, turn on some sexy MUSIC, you know how to play it . . .

We'll be up there in a few minutes or so.

So ENJOY IT, and we'll see you there my BEAUTIES!"

As Trish exits the stall - The Blond and Doe Angel can be heard LAUGHING and PLOTTING their sexy trap for Trish and her MAN . . .

AS Trish returns from the women's room, to Jack's private booth, with two fresh drinks just added on the table.

Jack's near drunk as he urges her to reveal her fantasy.

"Damn, where've you been?"

(As he looks into her eyes)

"You're STONED, aren't you Babe. . ."

Trish winks at him, then adds in her soft sensual voice.

"Did some Girl's Stuff, Jack?"

Trish then grabs the WINNINGS bag. . .

Let's get this haul up to YOUR room. Lock 'em in the SAFE, Jack! Then, we can go to my exotic SUITE and PART-TAY!"

Jack's caught in amazement by her new energy.

"Okay, Babe! But what's got into you, you're so erotically super-charged."

Trish continues in her sexy voice. . .

You'll see, Jack, You'll see. . . Just play along, COWBOY!"

LATER AT TRISH'S 'HIGH ROLLER' SUITE

VIBING to the MUSIC hard - Gabby and Doe Angel gyrate topless to the beat of NICKI MINAJ and ARIANA GRANDE'S 'BANG BANG'.

Clothes and Heels are scattered around the floor, and the bed sheets have already been WELL rustled.

Several FULL and HALF-EMPTY Champagne bottles and flutes are on a glass table with leftover coke dust spread across the top - nearby a reefer simmers in an ashtray.

We PAN the entire room. Then find Doe Angel pushing her hands into Gabby's black thong, as she slides it downward to the floor.

THEN

Trish and Jack suddenly APPEAR in the SUITE'S Doorway.

SEEING the scene of carnal frenzy, Trish quickly pulls off her silky top exposing her gorgeous breasts, as she kicks her heels to the side of the bed, then joins the DANCERS in a merge of flesh and moisture, grinding to the BANG BANG beat, together.

WATCHING in frozen ecstasy, Jack is so aroused just viewing this incredible scene of sexy bodies, he doesn't know where to begin, as they allure him with their hands and intoxicate him with their bodies and eyes to join in.

Gabby grabs Trish's naked breast, pulls her nipple and begins suckling her - WHILE Doe Angel pulls her own thong off, then quickly seizes Trish's short skirt along with her black 'Victoria Secrets' panties sliding them seductively down along her long legs to her ankles, as she moves her mouth down Trish's thighs -

Jack is clearly as HOT as he's ever been, as he too removes his own pants and shirt down to his black briefs.

In a trance-like gaze He enters the fray with abandon -

Trish melts into him first, then Gabby gets onto him tighter, finally Doe merges against his legs GRABBING his briefs in her mouth, as the DANCERS SEXUAL DELIRIUM EXPLODES onto HIM -

LATER THAT NIGHT - THE SECOND BEDROOM OF TRISH'S SUITE

As we drift through from the Main bedroom, only the light from the doorway guides us. The mirrors on the ceiling and walls reflect into the room -

AS

We SEE outlines at first, then two beautiful blond female forms lie naked on bare sheets across a king sized bed. They're either coked-out or physically exhausted.

On a bedside table - lines of coke on a glass top - an empty Champagne bottle and black lace panties, then, as we enter the Bathroom Jack has Doe Angel pinned against the marble sink, thrusting into her, hard - then viewing into the MIRROR, we see HER watching back at Jack's FACE in a euphoric coked out TRANCE -

Further back in the MIRROR, behind Jack at the DOORWAY, ENTERS Gabby naked - She grabs his ass and reaches around kissing him, as he PUMPS the tiny ass of Doe Angel, more violently now

Gabby's FACE moves down his back, and disappears from view

Doe stoned in a coke frenzy shouts. . .

"Let him go, Gabby!"

Then she screams in ecstasy.

"Harder, Jack, harder!"

(As she begins groaning)

"He's gonna go, Gabby. . . Let him release, Gabby!

"No, No, grab him harder...squeeze him hard!"

Suddenly Doe's orgasm erupts all over his crotch.

"OH MY GAWD, Gabby!" Gabby releases Jack, just as he erupts all over Doe, then Gabby screams.

"OH MY GAWD, Jack!"

Jack grunts out, his eyes searching for Trish,

"GAWD, GAWD, GAWD!"

SUDDENLY, IN THE MIRROR for all to see, Doe's FACE - her ORGASM takes over and Jack's EYES move in a FRENZY,

WE SEE the top of Gabby's blond hair covered with semen as she stays below Jack's waist, out of VIEW -

Jack WATCHES the whole SCENE as he grabs both Doe's breasts, thrusting again harder into Doe, then finally

LOOKING INTO THE MIRROR he spies Trish stoned, disheveled and naked, entering behind him,

Trish moves to Gabby - their LIPS MEET - their tongues slide seductively around while they continue kissing sensuously. . .but Trish is really watching Jack,

AS

Jack again begins GRINDING with crushing strength into Doe, knowing Trish is watching him in the MIRROR; and he knows from her eyes, she's getting intense carnal pleasure from it.

EARLY MORNING - THE MAIN BEDROOM OF TRISH'S SUITE

BLACK OUT CURTAINS hide the early morning sunrise trying to cut through the CURTAIN closures, as ARIANA GRANDE SONGS continue to PLAY softly in the background.

The bed here is even bigger than the King in the SECOND BEDROOM

Jack and Trish LAY naked on the sheets of the massive KING.

ALONE after their NIGHT of lascivious promiscuity with Doe and Gabby.

Jack lifts Trish up to kiss her breasts SUCKLING each nipple with finesse, as she finally again starts responding by thrusting her hips against him in a sexual FRENZY -

Trish arches her back and moves up to his mouth, grabbing his lip with her teeth, then bites hard and draws blood

AS

Jack is caught by surprise. . .

"DAMN, Trish . . .

Wipes his lip, then looks into her moist, deep blue EYES.

"WHAT was that for?"

Trish in a soft sexy tone of jealous love . . .

"You know, YOU SEXY BASTARD. . .

YOU couldn't wait to FUCK that Young Doe Angel.

Thought I was asleep in the back bedroom, didn't YOU!

Trish laughs . . . "HAH, I caught you!

YOU rode her tiny ass, HARD, YOU DIRTY MAN!

AND She hasn't even had her Twenty-first Birthday yet, WHAT A SEXY LECHEROUS MAN YOU ARE!"

Jack plays along with her fake jealousy . . .

"DAMN, Trish, you set me up for her and Gabby!

Look how wet you are now, just thinking about it, hard nipples and all!"

Jack smoothly enters her and starts pumping her again, this time, HARDER.

"YOU watched us all and enjoyed it, too!"

Trish gives him a lustful laugh, then grinds hard as she rolls over on top of him, their bodies move in unison responding to the stimulation.

"ACTUALLY, I LOVED IT, Jack!" She screams out in pleasure!

"FUCK ME, Jack, FUCK ME HARDER!"

Trish's mouth returns to Jacks lips as she wildly begins kissing him and licking off any blood she drew, just moments before.

MUCH LATER - MAIN BEDROOM OF TRISH'S SUITE

Still naked, Jack and Trish are lying relaxed on the massive KING. Light is now pushing through the cracks in the black-out curtains, when WE FOCUS ON TRISH'S FACE

AS

Her cellphone starts buzzing LOUDLY. She doesn't answer.

"OH GAWD, What TIME IS IT, Jack?"

Jack jumps off the bed and yells. . .

"DAMN, It's almost NOON, Trish!"

Trish reacts in panic.

"OH GAWD, That's my Cameraman?"

Trish jumps up, runs to the shower and yells back to him.

"I've got a One o'clock INTERVIEW, Jack!"

Jack moves to the second bedroom to get his clothes.

"LET'S get going, then!

SEE You in the LOBBY in fifteen, Trish!"

PART THREE

The Final Folly

Chapter 12

THE INTERVIEW

THE QUALLA POLICE STATION

Jack pulls the Blacked-Out SUV into a VISITOR Parking slot, near the ENTRANCE to THE QUALLA POLICE STATION -

He remains in the SUV as usual, while Trish jumps out, Cell in Hand, shouting at someone on-line

AS

She ENTERS the STATION, but NO ONE is around -

SHE ENTERS another OFFICE and STARES blankly at the QUALLA Boundary and Reservation Map on the wall, then glances around, as she continues talking on her Cell -

Trish on cell, reacts angry on the CELL CALL. . .

"Damn it, Larry, You, said you would be here by ONE!

Do you have all your camera gear?

Okay, Okay, You're Twenty minutes out!"

Trish moves to a another doorway inside the STATION.

"JUST get here, Larry, I've got a One o'clock INTERVIEW with Chief Vann, And that's NOW!"

SHE looks through the second DOORWAY into another OFFICE, but still NO ONE APPEARS in the room.

Trish walks through that OFFICE into a smaller ROOM and STOPS at what appears to be a COMPUTER AND PRINTER SPACE

A Young WOMAN in a sexy pastel tank top, low rider jeans and black heels with long black hair is bent over a FAX machine with I-PHONE plugs in her ears - she looks familiar

AS

Startled, Doe Angel turns and grabs OUT her I-PHONE plugs - off balance, but smiling as SHE realizes WHO it is behind her in full view. . .

"GAWD! Trish. . .

What are YOU doing here?"

Trish also reacts, but with shock and concern.

"DAMN, Doe, It's you!

You work HERE, at the Cherokee Police Station?"

Doe now very obviously friendly. . .

"Damn right! Trish. . .

Chief Vann's my BOSS, and my UNCLE, too!

Finally, Trish relaxes, as she feels even safer now.

"I'm here to interview him! Chief Vann, that is,

On The alleged FONTANA murder case. It's supposed to be at one o'clock."

Doe reacts sad, then amazed.

"Well. . . The Chief had an Emergency up on the North end of the Reservation!

Sorry, Trish. . .

So you're a 'REAL TV' Celebrity!"

Trish is caught smiling at that comment.

"Well, not exactly, Doe! I'm just a Field Reporter for a Knoxville Based News Station, WKNX,

We need to follow-up on some details in this Murder Case!"

Doe is suddenly feeling in control of the situation.

"Well, GAWD, Trish. . .

I can tell you more about that CASE than he can -

Besides, He's a pretty MEAN INDIAN and he'll just tell you it's Privileged information -

and still under investigation: The Typical BULLSHIT."

Trish thinks, 'WOW, we just hit the jackpot'!

"Well, seriously Doe, 'Off the Record', What CAN, you tell me?"

"I'll tell you one thing right off, Trish.

It's no longer an Alleged MURDER CASE.

The Coroner, 'Doc Bull', gave me a document this morning.

I was just faxing it down to Asheville. . .

TO Guess WHO?"

Trish is all ears. . .

"Who, Doe?" Doe smiles with an impish grin.

"That sexy Blond Beauty we FUCKED last night, Gabby!

She's the State's Assistant District Attorney, for our District."

Trish goes nuts with laughter!

"WOW. that's a HOOT, and what a Beauty she is too!

GAWD, she knows how to FUCK!

And DANCE. . .

Damn, I love Gabby's tits!"

Doe, suddenly becomes very emotional. . .

"I love Gabby too, Trish, but she gambles too much,

And she's always half broke when she comes up here from Asheville! I always give her some of my personal allocation of QUALLA NATION chips, whenever she visits.

Sometimes, it's over a thousand-dollars-worth!"

Trish exudes equal emotional empathy. . .

"That's really, really sad, Doe!"

Trish pauses to think about her plight, then is serious again.

"So, Doe, What DID, the Coroner's Report Say?"

Now Doe is feeling back in control again, willing and excited.

"Okay, Trish. . .

Here's what you need to know, Doc Bull, said in his report that the State's DNA proved the CORPSE WAS a CHEROKEE INDIAN, AND that he died from a series of EXPLOSIVE SHRAPNEL bullets fired directly into his chest.

Plus, those bullets were likely Military Issue and considered major TOP SECRET back then, and restricted until the late 1960's.

Trish in reality shock. . .

"Oh my GAWD, that's incredible!"

Suddenly, they HEAR someone entering the STATION DOOR.

Doe Angel rushes off to the FRONT OFFICE, as Trish sees several evidence documents, including the CORONER's ID DOCUMENTS, indicating WHO the MAN WAS.

She PHOTOS the DOCS with her I-PHONE, just as it buzzes.

She checks the ID with a scowl on her face. . .

"What's up now, Larry?

"Wait Outside in the Van, I'll be there in Five!"

In moments, Doe Angel returns from the FRONT OFFICE with no NEWS about the Chief, as she instinctively grabs Trish's face, then hesitates before she kisses her on the lips.

"I hope I've helped you, Trish. I've got to get back to work since our QUALLA RESERVATION CHIEF is in the Office now, but Call me, soon!"

(Doe puts her number in Trish's phone)

Trish is also, sincerely emotional. . .

"You have, Doe! You have no idea!

And, I'll call you soon, don't worry."

Doe looks at Trish concerned, as she adds. . .

"OH, and Trish, I have a serious surprise for you.

Officer Andrew Black Hawk, just showed up at the front OFFICE entrance and I've asked him to take you up to the MURDERED MAN'S Cabin."

(Doe then hands Trish a document)

"He's waiting for you, but you must hurry, since he's only OFF-DUTY 'til Four!

Good Luck, Love!"

Doe reacts again, as she again hugs Trish.

LARGE BLACK MURDERED-OUT CHEVY SUV

Very shocked and aroused by what he's heard inside, Jack's EYES have been fixed on his NSA NAV SCREEN MONITOR, during Trish's entire visit as he completes picking up and notating all the AUDIO ACTION inside the QUALLA STATION!

The Qualla Boundary

Above Fontana Dam

OUTSIDE the FRONT DOOR of the QUALLA POLICE STATION A LARGE OFFICER STANDS at the DOORWAY just as Trish EXITS reading the Document Doe Angel gave her. IT'S OFFICER ANDREW BLACK HAWK.

She greets him and asks him to wait just a few minutes, before she's ready to go.

She then walks directly over to the WKNX CAMERA VAN parked nearby, opens the rear door and disappears inside.

Jack quickly re-energizes the NSA NAV SCREEN MONITOR, to pick up Trish and her Cameraman's conversation inside the VAN.

WKNX CAMERA VAN

Trish hands Larry the document and Coroner photos. . .

"You've got to get all this to my Editor, Larry!"

Larry is now completely confused.

"What about the POLICE CHIEF INTERVIEW?"

Trish gets very serious.

"That, can wait! This has got to get on the NEWS DESK, by tonight, Larry!"

Trish pointing through the dashboard window, to Officer Black Hawk standing outside.

"You see that BIG MAN at the door. . .

This document says he's a relative of the MURDERED INDIAN. And now, he's gonna take me to his GREAT UNCLE'S old Cabin in the Mountains, to see what that Indian's personal belongings were.

This is the big break we've needed to uncover the REAL REASONS WHY this man was MURDERED!

Oh, and Larry. . .

I know you're Fucking my 'Gofer GAL', so don't stop in MARYVILLE tonight, For a QUICKIE with her!

This must get to Bill Berman, now!"

LARGE BLACK MURDERED-OUT CHEVY SUV

Jack's EYES ARE GLUED ON his NAS NAV SCREEN MONITOR once again, as he listens to Trish and Larry review the DOC and I-Photos she's taken from inside the POLICE STATION.

But unfortunately, the NAV FEED also alerts ALSOS HEADQUARTERS, AS a SECOND MONITOR WINDOW in the SUV's main NAV SCREEN lights up.

WASHINGTON DC - ENERGY DEPT. SECRET WORK ROOM

Jack's NAV DATA is being received on a selected VIDEO SCREEN - ALL OTHER AGENTS and OPERATIVES are busy on other monitors and workstations - the ROOM is buzzing.

DC based ALSOS General Anderson, switches on his remote controlled screen to watch Jack in his SUV, as we see several SUITED ALSOS OPERATIVES just like Jack, ready to fly out to North Carolina and Tennessee.

They're also viewing the Monitor around the table with the General, as he speaks to Jack in a vicious tone of voice.

"...Jack, looks like your TARGET is about to spill the beans on this one. . . Maybe it's CLEANUP TIME?

Jack Wolcott has his pro-hat on but he's very concerned how to handle Trish and the assignment.

"We need to Follow it to CONCLUSION, General!

Still don't know all the PLAYERS, if we want the loose ends really CLEANED UP!"

Anderson speaks. . .

"Up to now, I have Agreed! But that WKNX Cameraman, MUST GO, before he gets that INFO to the NATIONAL MEDIA!"

Anderson is agitated and loud as he adds . . .

"YOU CLEAN the RESERVATION PEOPLE and that REPORTER!

We'll take care of the collateral damage in ASHEVILLE and KNOXVILLE! CLEAR!"

Jack is on edge as Trish is returning to the SUV.

"CLEAR, General!

GOT TO GO! The GIRL'S on her way to my SUV!"

Jack REPOSITIONS the NSA NAV SCREEN MONITORS and prepares the ruse, just as Trish Freeman RE-ENTERS the SUV. . .

ALL is back in place and READY - Jack smiles at Trish as she slides into her seat, leaning over to kiss his cheek.

Trish pulsing with excitement. . .

"You won't believe who I met in the POLICE STATION, Jack!

Jack back in character.

"Tell me, Babe!"

And, what happened at your Interview?"

Trish is energized. . .

"Don't worry about that 'Damn' Interview, Jack!

What I'm about to say, BLOWS all of that away!

But before I tell you,

(She points to the OFFICER)

That poor man waiting over there, is Officer Andrew Black Hawk, and he's gonna take us up to a Place, that will get my real STORY!

Trish OPENS her door and gives Andrew Black Hawk the GO-AHEAD WAVE, then returns into the SUV.

"Follow his POLICE CAR, Jack!"

In ACTION, JACK'S SUV squeals out of the parking lot, tightly behind the QUALLA POLICE CAR heading to possibly, HER FINAL ANSWER!

Chapter 13

THE SHAMAN'S CABIN

NEAR A DENSE MOUNTAIN OVERLOOK ON FONTANA LAKE

DRIVING HARD up roughly paved and winding roads into the Mountains above the CHEROKEE NATION, Jack quickly follows the QUALLA OFFICER to a densely wooded area overlooking a massive lake, FONTANA LAKE

HERE the Road turns to gravel, then dirt, then large rocks and weeds.

AFTER about thirty more minutes, they ARRIVE.

TALL CANADIAN PINE TREES and thick BRUSH hide the area from VIEW and the ENTRANCE ROAD. The CABIN itself is in major disrepair, but sits wedged into the hillside on a sturdy foundation of stone and concrete with a small metal door on the basement side. ITS LOCKED.

Officer Andrew Black Hawk angles his POLICE CAR at the CABIN ENTRANCE and EXITS as JACK'S SUV pulls up beside it.

The Officer unlatches a LARGE WOOD DOOR at the FRONT of the CABIN, then moves inside without acknowledging ANYONE.

Trish Freeman opens HER Door, scared, but excited as she EXITs the SUV. . .

"You stay here, Jack!"

Jack reaches his hand out of the CAR DOOR with something to give HER and SHOUTS as she WALKS away . . .

Trish seems surprised, nervous. . .

"What is it, Jack?"

"It's a PAGER!"

Just press it, if you need me!"

Trish stuffs it into HER PURSE -

Then without any hesitation OR outward FEAR

SHE ENTERS through the dark DOORWAY of the CABIN.

INSIDE THE MURDERED-OUT SUV

Jack QUICKLY ACTIVATES the PAGER and begins OBSERVING her with the NSA NAV SYSTEM

EYES ON THE NAV SCREEN as Jack MANIPULATES an OVERLAY MAP showing the QUALLA BOUNDARY to CONFIRM their location near FONTANA LAKE.

THEN, HE WAITS. . .

INSIDE THE RUNDOWN CABIN - NEAR OLD FONTANA

The HUGE HULK of Officer Andrew Black Hawk shadows the only window in the ROOM,

Trish nearly smashes into his MASSIVE BODY as her eyes TRANSITION from the BRIGHT outside SUNLIGHT to the UNLIT CABIN INTERIOR.

Trish is shocked with fear as she reacts. . .

"Oh my GAWD, Officer Black Hawk,

(She catches her breath)

I didn't mean to bump YOU, I couldn't see anything, It's the outside glare!"

The MUSTY SMELL of the CABIN merged with the odd SMELL of Officer Black Hawk almost chokes her, as Trish pushes some cobwebs aside and waits for any indication from the HULK.

"Are there any LIGHTS in HERE?"

SUDDENLY, Officer Black Hawk ignites his FLASHLIGHT BEAM at a Lantern on a corner TABLE near a dusty CHEST OF DRAWERS.

HE goes to IT, POPS OPEN A ZIPPO - LIGHTS IT

Then, TURNS to Trish in a deep voice, almost foreboding.

"YOU PEOPLE, should NOT be up HERE - THIS IS SACRED INDIAN GROUND!

Doe Angel, said to take YOU, so now you should KNOW . . .

That CORPSE was my GREAT UNCLE, A CHEROKEE NATION SHAMAN,

To YOU WHITE'S, he was a MINING ENGINEER . . .

HE KNEW TO MUCH, SO THEY KILLED HIM!

Trish responds cautious. . .

"Officer Black Hawk, I have always been in SYMPATHY for the sufferings of your CHEROKEE NATION . . .

So, please don't judge me with other whites!

I truly feel your pain! And through this effort,

We will uncover the truth to RIGHT this horrible MURDER, and what it has done to your PEOPLE.

Trish waits silently for his response, THERE IS NONE.

She's still very careful of his reaction. To her questions.

"Officer Black Hawk, can you show me what Doe Angel wanted me to see?"

Officer Black Hawk again ignites his FLASHLIGHT BEAM - POINTS IT to the dusty CHEST OF DRAWERS, then growls his words.

"Pull out that chest!

There's a TRAP DOOR under it;

A SAFE under that . . .

There, will be your ANSWER!"

Trish rushes over to the CHEST OF DRAWERS and struggles to push it aside. So, Black Hawk grabs her arm and moves THE CHEST for her.

On the FLOOR under it is a TRAP DOOR almost invisible and matching the Floor slats perfectly. It's massive, large enough for her to crawl into, once opened.

SHE follows his instructions, until the TRAP is OPENED and she faces what looks like a Nineteen-Twenty's styled BANK VAULT mounted below the floor boards.

THE LARGE DOOR has a steel handle, a simple circular numbered DIAL, and A CHEROKEE NATION EAGLE emblazoned on its surface

Trish is really excited . . .

"What now, Officer Black Hawk? It's LOCKED!"

The HUGE INDIAN aims his LIGHT BEAM at the SAFE DIAL -

And barks his answer. . .

"He was, WA YA, THE WOLF - His LAND was of The WOLF -

HIS CLAN was of The WOLF -

AND as THE WOLF, HE ALONE GUARDS the SACRED GOLD of OUR NATION'S CREATOR, U NET LAN VHI -

We once had SEVEN CLANS -

WOLF, Deer, Bird, Longhair, Wild Potato, Blue, and Paint!

These SEVEN CLANS of our Nation, will be his CODE 7-7-7!"

WITHOUT hesitating Trish tries the NUMBERS

SHE moves the DIAL - LEFT then RIGHT, then several other ways UNTIL CLICK - SHE PULLS the SAFE'S HANDLE, it OPENS with hydraulics

Trish, then stares into its depth, as the HULK Points his LIGHT BEAM into the SAFE, revealing a single BOOK lying on a SOLID METAL DOOR with another Handle and a Key Slot, that hides even MORE SECRETS. IT'S LOCKED.

CHEROKEE SYMBOLS ADORN the book's weathered cover.

Trish turns to the HULK. . .

"Can I TOUCH IT?

(She, clears her throat)

"I mean, THE BOOK?"

Officer Black Hawk STEPS over HER nervous body - Reaches down to GRAB the BOOK, PULLING the lower METAL DOOR Handle to confirm that it's LOCKED and SECURE -

Then RE-LATCHES the MAIN SAFE DOOR and spins the DIAL AS HE HANDS the Book to Trish, like a GENTLE GIANT.

EXCITED - SHE HOLDS IT like a precious sacred ancient artifact,

UNTIL she OPENS IT, and realizes it's THE WOLFE SHAMAN'S DIARY, and it's NOT written in ENGLISH

It's scribed in THE CHEROKEE WRITTEN LANGUAGE OF SYMBOLS!

AGAIN, the HUGE INDIAN aims his LIGHT BEAM, this time at the BOOK -

Officer Black Hawk's look seems ominous, as he gives her a serious warning. . .

"Doe Angel says, AWINITA VAN will translate this for you -

After that, I must take this BOOK to be buried with my GREAT UNCLE, THE WOLF SHAMAN'S EARTHLY BODY. . .

WA YA, must be BURIED in THE DAWN -

We will go now to Doe Angel and she will take you to Awinita. . .

But, we must hurry!"

Chapter 14

AWINITA VAN

SOMEWHERE IN THE CHEROKEE NATION - NIGHT

KITUWAH ACADEMY

A RIVER rushes nearby as RAIN begins to leave mist and fog in the trees, as it moves upward into the towering Mountains above

NEARBY, a large 1950's GOVERNMENT styled brick building and a deserted PARKING LOT except for JACK'S SUV, Doe Angel's old FORD PICK-UP TRUCK and a CHEVY SEDAN, all are located in Front. Lights can be seen in a back office

AS

Trish and Doe Angel - PUSH-THROUGH the entrance and ENTER

A long hallway dimly lit. It's in a Private School - a bilingual Cherokee and English language immersion School for the Eastern Cherokee Reservation,

THEY WALK QUICKLY

Finally, a DOORWAY - beside it a wooden plaque READS

'AWINITA FAWN VAN - HEAD INSTRUCTOR'

THEY ENTER without knocking. . .

AWINITA'S OFFICE

A hard older woman with long black hair, Facial features similar to Doe Angel, but BLACK piercing EYES WATCHES them, as they quietly SIT in front of her desk.

Doe Angel speaks first, (IN THE CHEROKEE LANGUAGE)

"I have been missing you GREATLY, MY SACRED SISTER.

I bring My LOVE to YOU and YOUR CHILDREN."

Awinita Van responds to her, (IN THE CHEROKEE LANGUAGE)

"AND TO YOU, LITTLE SISTER, MY LOVE AS WELL.

AND this is the ONE YOU called ABOUT. . . AND WHO IS SHE?

Doe Angel speaks, (AGAIN IN THE CHEROKEE LANGUAGE)

"SHE IS MY FRIEND AND SOMEONE WE CAN TRUST WITH HER TRUTH."

Doe turns to Trish. . .

"Trish, this is my SACRED SOUL SISTER,

SHE is a GREAT TEACHER of our CHEROKEE NATION - AND A MEMBER OF THE QUALLA COUNCIL - Awinita Van.

Trish is clearly reverent and sensitive as she speaks,

"Such a pleasure to meet you, Madam Van."

Awinita Van responds to her in a friendly tone.

"YOU may call me Awinita, FRIEND!"

Then she turns to Doe Angel.

"So, MY LOVE. What can I do for you two LADIES, at this late hour?"

Doe Angel removes THE BOOK from her large PURSE BAG, and carefully places it in front of Awinita on the desk -

Doe speaks again, (IN THE CHEROKEE LANGUAGE)

"This belongs to BLACK HAWK WOLFE, it's his GREAT UNCLE'S DIARY. . .

WE NEED IT TRANSLATED TO ENGLISH AND RETURNED TO BLACK HAWK WOLFE! THEY WILL BURY HIS BODY AND THIS DIARY, ON THEIR LAND AT DAWN."

Awinita Van responds, (IN THE CHEROKEE LANGUAGE)

"OH YES - THE SHAMAN WA YA!

(VAN HIDES HER FEELINGS)

"A MYSTERIOUS MAN - HE HAD A BAD REPUTATION WITH OUR COUNCIL.

MY BROTHER SAID THE BODY WAS THE CORPSE from FONTANA

INSIDE THE MURDERED-OUT SUV

AGAIN, Jack is squirming with SERIOUS CONCERNS - TOO MANY TARGETS - as he works his NAS NAV MONITORING SYSTEM, KNOWING all the time, that Anderson is also monitoring these CONVERSATIONS and taking dangerous ACTIONS of his own.

SOMEWHERE NEARBY

Another SUV with head lamps out, PARKS out of sight - three FIGURES emerge and silently WALK toward a UTILITY BUILDING.

IN AWINITA'S OFFICE

Awinita looks at Trish, then Doe Angel -

"This TRANSLATION may take some time, would you rather me read it VERBALLY first. . .

Then I'll highlight the most important things out loud to you, in ENGLISH."

Trish opens her briefcase.

"Madam Van. . . Uh, Awinita, May I record this, As you READ it to us?"

Awinita nods okay at Trish. . .

SHE begins, as Trish LAUNCHES her Cell's RECORD APP

Awinita's VERBAL mumbling of words rapidly in the CHEROKEE Language, is the ONLY SOUND –

THEN, after a few moments she STOPS ABRUPTLY –

Awinita has a slight gasp, then she gets serious.

"He writes . . .OUR CHEROKEE LANDS

on EAGLE CREEK at the LITTLE TENNESSEE are filled with DEEP VEINS of GOLD

With very HIGH ASSAY values of ninety-seven percent purity. . . He's tested it – WA YA's tested it!"

Doe Angel interrupts excited. . .

"In today's World, Trish, that LAND is over Two-Hundred feet below the lake's SURFACE, at FONTANA."

Awinita continues still serious. . .

"He's INFORMED the OLD QUALLA COUNCIL that those LANDS will be covered by DEEP WATERS – they will be filled from a NEW GOVERNMENT DAM they will build in our LITTLE TENNESSEE VALLEY. The QUALLA COUNCIL asked him to go to WASHINGTON to plead for OUR NATION." (All of them are silent)

"Let me continue reading!"

AGAIN Awinita mumbles CHEROKEE SOUNDS rapidly, then SILENCE

Doe Angel interrupts again. . .

"What is it, SISTER What have you FOUND?"

Awinita has tears, then fear in her eyes as she speaks. . .

"He's SEES a POWERFUL MAN in WASHINGTON . . .

A GENERAL. . .

But they don't HEAR him, they say what he has, doesn't MATTER.

The LAND is CONTROLLED by something called

A-L-S-O-S and the DAM will be built for the WAR EFFORT, at ANY COST!

If he tells ANYONE or ANY of the thousands of MEN that will be sent for building the DAM PROJECT about the GOLD, it will cause a MASS stampede - a GOLD RUSH. . .

The DAM will NOT get BUILT in TIME to DESTROY NAZI GERMANY and JAPAN. And He, THE GENERAL, will ERADICATE OUR CHEROKEE NATION for this OFFENSE AGAINST the US GOVERNMENT'S PLAN.

ONCE AGAIN, 'AS IN THE TRAIL OF TEARS' THE GOVERNMENT WILL BE SENDING, THOSE LEFT ALIVE, AWAY to MONTANA RESERVATIONS or elsewhere

ALL QUALLA CHEROKEE will be FORCED TO LEAVE THESE SACRED LANDS FOREVER AND HE,

THE WOLFE SHAMAN, WA YA, will become A WAR SACRIFICE, NEVER to be heard from AGAIN!"

ALL AT ONCE, she gets up and URGENTLY WALKS to the Door -

Awinita is agitated, then clears her throat. . .

"I HEARD something, I must check on our COMPRESSOR ROOM, LADIES

(Secretly without observation, she grabs the DIARY)

"Please, STAY HERE, I'll be right back!"

Doe Angel is upset. . .

"Is there something else WRONG, Awinita?"

As the door closes. . . there's no answer.

BUT Awinita is GONE as Doe and Trish, both wait in SILENCE.

INSIDE THE MURDERED-OUT SUV

ON THE NAS NAV MONITOR SCREEN - Anderson in WASHINGTON and suddenly Thomas Macabe - ALSOS Main Headquarters - COULEE(HQ)

- ALL are screaming incoherently at Jack Wolcott

BUT, Jack Wolcott is NOT responding -

AS

INSIDE THE CHEROKEE KITUWAH ACADEMY BUILDING

LIGHTS begin flickering, then GO OUT

At first, Doe Angel and Trish are FROZEN in PLACE. Then together, they erupt in SCREAMS.

Instinctively, Trish reaches into her purse, GRABS JACK'S PAGER and PRESSES IT . . .

THEN

They BOTH LAUNCH their CELL PHONE FLASHLIGHT Apps

ALSOS HEADQUARTERS - WASHINGTON DC

Yuan is now desperate to reach Jack.

"This is MONARCH -

STATUS, NAV-ONE, STATUS, NAV-ONE! Code In!"

(Shaken - Yuan looks at Anderson)

"He's gone OFF-LINE, General"

General Anderson unhinged - He MOTIONS to ALERT two of his TOP FIELD OPERATIVES

(PURE Assassins - Fast and Dirty, not Clean Methods, like Jack Wolcott)

Anderson shows stark fear and loathing at once.

"He's OUT OF CONTROL - Take the JET"

Anderson gets LOUDER. . .

"YOU can use that LOCAL strip in MURPHY, North Carolina. IT'S 'VFR' VISUAL but the CITATION XLS can land on FIFTY-FIVE HUNDRED FEET in the DARK!

I want this thing CUT OUT, NOW!

I GAVE that SON-OF-BITCH, Sole CONTROL over the CHEROKEE JOB! Now we're SCREWED!

WELL. . . So is Jack Wolcott, THE BASTARD!"

Thomas Macabe's face burning with negative energy, at once, comes on the Main Monitor screen, as both OPERATIVES clear the room heading for their ASSIGNMENTS. . .

"Have we CLEANED this MESS YET! That SHIT in ASHEVILLE?

And that WKNX CAMERAMAN in KNOXVILLE?"

Macabe is gasping for air, he's so pissed. . .

"IF we're not CONTAINED General - YOU'RE a DEAD MAN!"

Anderson knows he's done for anyhow. . .

"ASHEVILLE as we speak, SIR!"

THE STATE ATTORNEY'S OFFICE - ASHEVILLE NC

The entire floor is EMPTY of workers, hardly any lights are on - IT'S LATE

Gabby is working her COMPUTER SCREEN - feverishly she makes notes about the details from the FAX sent from CHEROKEE regarding THE FONTANA CORPSE -

ON THE COMPUTER SCREEN, then, ON HER FACE, she sips her coffee

AS

ATTORNEY'S OFFICE KITCHEN - SAME TIME

Nearby in a small Kitchen Work Room next door, an ALSOS OPERATIVE prepares a specialized REMOTE Gas

Explosion Amplifier Device. Then DISAPPEARS into the darkness of the Hallway

INSTANTLY

The CITY BUILDING's Fourth FLOOR, ERUPTS in a MASSIVE

EXPLOSION with FLAMES BOILING OUT of Offices, Windows, everywhere. . . NOTHING can survive this.

CHAOS, Just as planned!

ALSOS HEADQUARTERS - WASHINGTON DC

Yuan chimes in behind the General. . .

"ASHEVILLE just called in, SIR! IT'S DONE...

KNOXVILLE is in PROGRESS!"

Anderson acknowledges, as he frantically WAVES a crazy hand motion to his two TOP FIELD OPERATIVES - still holding for HIS ORDERS

"GO! GO! GO! - OUT OF HERE!"

Anderson turns to Yuan. . .

"MONARCH, GET KNOXVILLE - WE need a STATUS CIPHER, NOW!

IMMEDIATELY, MONARCH does a relay on his NAS NAV Screen to his KNOXVILLE Field Operatives, then waits for contact. . .

"STATUS UPDATE! Code-In!"

TRAILER PARK OUTSIDE MARYVILLE, TENNESSEE

DOUBLE WIDE TRAILER

Inside the TRAILER, two SHADOWY FIGURES ENTER and move down a narrow hallway past a bathroom, to the open doorway of a BEDROOM

WE LOOK SLOWLY INTO THE BEDROOM - TWO NAKED BODIES

It's Larry, the WKNX CAMERAMAN and his beautiful young 'Gofer Gal' from WKNX thrusting in a frenzy of flesh. She grinds her hips down onto him - he grabs her breasts and faces into her eyes - violently thrusting into her. HE SHOULDN'T BE HERE!

OBLIVIOUS TO EVERYTHING AROUND THEM WE SEE THE SHADOWY FIGURES ENTER THE ROOM

TWO TRANQUILIZER DARTS are SILENTLY FIRED into the COUPLE!

Larry and the 'Gofer Gal' collapse on the bed. They don't know what hit them.

NOTHING MOVES as the TWO FIGURES place a specialized REMOTE Explosive Device in the Kitchen. Then exit outside

One of the FIGURES drives off in LARRY'S WKNX VAN

The other FIGURE enters a BLACKED OUT CHEVY SUV, then drives just to the entrance of the sleeping TRAILER PARK

IN MOMENTS

The WALLS of the DOUBLE WIDE seem to IMPLODE,

THEN BELCHOUTWARD, while the entire TRAILER'S remains lift high into the air and, IN SLOW MOTION, fall back into THE TOWERING FLAMES

ALARMS GO OFF, all around the TRAILER PARK.

ALSOS HEADQUARTERS - WASHINGTON DC

Yuan accepts their response. . .

"KNOXVILLE'S DONE, SIR!"

(Yuan, without emotion)

"WHAT are your ORDERS, SIR!"

Anderson is still desperate, still wants Jack ON-LINE. . .

"PULL UP NAV-ONE, AGAIN, NOW!"

(Anderson turns to Rita)

"RUN a systems check on his NAVS"

Rita responds,

"IT'S ALL GREEN, SIR!

He's just NOT INSIDE our VEHICLE. Nothing is SHUT DOWN.

The SUV is running, GPS and ALL SYSTEMS are UP"

Suddenly Yuan himself, tries urgently to reach Jack.

"STATUS, NAV-ONE, STATUS, NAV-ONE! CODE-IN"

(Yuan, cautiously calls out to Anderson)

"He's NOT ANSWERING, General, ON-BOARD or REMOTE"

Rita then shouts to Anderson. . .

"CORRECTION, SIR! He's now CODE RED!

He's just SHUT DOWN the VEHICLE!"

Anderson instantly become crazy mad. . .

"DAMN, that SOB, I'm GOING!"

The General turns to Blanc. . .

"Blanc, HOLD that CITATION! AND get ME on it, NOW!"

Then He turns back to Yuan before leaving. . .

"You've got OPERATIONS, MONARCH!"

Yuan tries to reason with him. . .

"General, what are you doing? Macabe will go NON-LINEAR!"

BUT before MONARCH can finish, General Anderson has grabbed his gear and is OUT the DOOR -

What is left is MONARCH'S SHOCKED FACE. . .

HE's Exasperated.

YET now, He's IN-CHARGE.

AS once again, MONARCH desperately tries to REACH Jack Wolcott, a man he has always respected, for the last ten years. But where is he and can he survive the massed ALSOS TEAMS HEADING HIS WAY.

Chapter 15

THE UTILITY BUILDING REVEAL

KITUWAH SCHOOL PARKING LOT - CHEROKEE

Jack MOVES SILENTLY in a Tree Line along the RIVER'S EDGE in STEALTH GEAR with night vision goggles.

THE SOUND of the RUSHING WATER over the shallow rapids, blocks all NOISE, as he FOCUSES on the TARGET'S hidden SUV in the shadows.

HE SURVEYS the vehicle - PERMANENT STATE TAGS, a barely apparent CHEROKEE CASINO ID sticker on the left windshield, a RADIO MOUNT on the lower dashboard and more obvious, a large black LOCK BOX for GUNS, AMMO or SOMETHING in its cargo area.

He saw the LIGHTS GO OUT IN THE SCHOOL and shifts position . . .

TO

THE UTILITY BUILDING

Suddenly a WOMAN quickly EXITS the SCHOOL BUILDING - SHE RUNS to the UTILITY BUILDING DOORWAY, turns to look back then ENTERS.

Jack quickly moves to the building and mounts a
NAS SENSOR on the BUILDING WALL

AS WE SEE JACK LISTENING (EAR PLUGS) - THEN WE
VIEW INSIDE THE BUILDING, as Awinita expresses
herself in a mad and very agitated reaction. . .

"WHAT took you so long?"

THE CASINO SECURITY MAN reacts viscously back
towards her. . .

"FUCK YOU TOO, BITCH!

BOSS told you, to GET that DIARY, before the FEDS
GRAB IT!

And NOW you're SPILLING its GUTS to a TV
NEWSWOMAN!"

Awinita responds equally viscous. . .

"I'M here, YOU ASSHOLE, because I found SOMETHING
in the TRANSLATION.

I Didn't tell those WOMEN any more than they
needed to know!

WHAT no one KNOWS, 'til NOW, is SHAMAN WOLFE
built a SMELTING FORGE in the basement of HIS
CABIN. HE mined and collected GOLD off the
surface land, as much GOLD as he could, then he
transformed all of it into ONE POUND BULLION
BARS, HUNDREDS of THEM, ENGRAVED with the EAGLE
of our CHEROKEE NATION on each BAR.

They're STORED in his VAULT, somewhere in THE
SHAMAN's old CABIN - PROBLEM is . . . WE don't
know EXACTLY where his CABIN is actually located.

Without Doe Angel bringing me that NEWSWOMAN, so I could TRANSLATE the DIARY - Officer Black Hawk would NEVER have revealed its whereabouts or LOANED the DIARY to Doe Angel!

DID YOU or THE BOSS even know THAT!

Black Hawk is one of the LAST BRAVES of the WOLFE CLAN and NO ONE KNOWS where HE and HIS FAMILY have buried their DEAD. . . OR

WHERE they'll bury his GREAT UNCLE, the one who actually SCRIBED THIS!"

SHE lifts up the DIARY into his face.

"THIS DIARY would never have seen the light of Day, without ME, you idiot!

IT would have been BURIED, with the GREAT UNCLE, Wa Ya!

You can tell that to the COUNCIL. . .

And to Chief Yona too, for ME personally!"

SUDDENLY, OUT of the DARK SHADOWS STEPS, Council Chief Yona

Yona faces her with retribution in his eyes. . .

"YOU can tell him yourself, Awinita!

That's HUNDREDS OF MILLIONS of DOLLARS in hidden GOLD BULLION BARS and a SHAMAN'S DIARY!

ALL of it belongs to the TRIBE, The COUNCIL,

And the QUALLA NATION. . .

The WOLFE CLAN will HOARD IT for their OWN. . .

But it MUST be shared with THE CHEROKEE NATION!"

Awinita responds equally viscous emotion. . .

"You mean YOU ALONE, YOU GREEDY BASTARD!"

OUTSIDE THE SCHOOL UTILITY BUILDING

Jack continues LISTENING, but his EARPHONE also picks up Trish's URGENT PAGER SIGNALS.

At that moment, He focuses on the SCHOOL BUILDING DOORWAY . . .

It's OPENING, as both Trish and Doe Angel's FLASHLIGHT BEAMS strike the UTILITY ROOM DOORWAY and they begin moving towards it. . .

(Jack silently, to himself)

"Oh Shit, Ladies, What NOW. . . Looks like you leave me no choice!"

Jack purposely THUMPS the BUILDING sidewall, then MELTS silently back into the shadows

AS

A CASINO SECURITY MAN reacts on alert. . .

"SOMEONE'S Outside . . ."

Inside, Awinita immediately points to the door.

"BOLT that door, they're COMING! And SOMEONE get the power back on, now!"

INSIDE THE UTILITY BUILDING

The CASINO SECURITY MAN LOCKS the Utility Door and MOTIONS to the back of the room, where a THIRD MAN, previously hidden from view, throws the CIRCUIT BREAKERS back ON. Illumination from the OUTSIDE SECURITY LIGHTS, FLOODS into the ROOM through a WINDOW - but the INTERIOR remains mostly in shadows

OUTSIDE THE UTILITY BUILDING

Trish and Doe Angel are at first stunned by the sudden GLARE of the overhead SECURITY LAMPS

AS

Doe Angel GRABS the UTILITY DOOR KNOB - IT'S LOCKED. . .

Doe at once, starts BANGING the door. . .

"Awinita. . . Are you in THERE? Come OUT HERE, Awinita!

Trish and Doe Angel go SILENT, as they WAIT

INSIDE

Awinita in a low voice, motions the Men away. . .

"Get your Men out of sight, Chief Yona!

I'll handle these BITCHES - And remember,

They don't know ANYTHING yet - So let's keep it that way!

Awinita turns - WALKS to the DOOR and UN-BOLTS it.

OUTSIDE

Doe Angel is REALLY NERVOUS. . . She HEARS MOVEMENT and again starts BANGING. . .

"Awinita, we're WAITING . . . We know you have the DIARY!"

INSIDE/OUTSIDE THE BUILDING DOORWAY

Awinita slowly pushes the UTILITY DOOR OPEN and MOVES toward Doe Angel.

Doe Angel is incensed, her mouth wide open. . .

"What WERE you thinking, Awinita? You took the DIARY, then the LIGHTS went out. We were left in the DARK!"

Awinita reacts and fakes 'very apologetic'. . .

'I'm embarrassed, Doe Angel.

When I heard that SOUND - 'IT WAS THE COMPRESSOR'

I had to get back here, QUICKLY, but the BREAKER Kicked Off, before I could get to it - I LOCKED the door for SECURITY REASONS.

Just an AUTOMATIC reaction, I guess - and grabbing the DIARY, too . . .

I'm so sorry."

Trish and Doe Angel's FACES are AGHAST, YET, they both seem to accept her limp EXPLANATION.

ALL of THEM, SPEECHLESS and IN SHOCK, RETURN back into the SCHOOL BUILDING.

Jack LOOKS out of the shadows and BREATHES a sigh of RELIEF, as he WATCHES the three women, DISAPPEAR into the SCHOOL DOORWAY

THEN, He returns to LISTENING, against the UTILITY ROOM WALL,

AS

Chief Yona nervously whispers to his Casino Security Man.

"That was CLOSE!

But I want, both those SQUAWS GONE, before this night is over!"

The Casino Security Man reacts surprised. . .

"Doe Angel, too . . . She's the only one that knows where Black Hawk's CABIN is!"

Chief Yona reacts frustrated and violent. . .

"Then beat it out of her; threaten her!

And make sure it's an ACCIDENT - use her Truck - You know the Drill!

Doe Angel, and that News-Bitch, get it done before this night is over!

I'll deal with Awinita, Later!"

OUTSIDE THE UTILITY BUILDING DOORWAY

Jack HEARS the UTILITY DOOR LATCH OPEN, as all three Men EMERGE, The Council Chief MOTIONS to the THIRD MAN (Little Foot)

Chief Yona turns to his Security man. . .

"You stay here and get it done!"

(Chief Yona walks toward his SUV)

"And you're with me, Little Foot!"

Jack WATCHES the Casino Security Man MOVE toward the SCHOOL PARKING LOT,

While Chief Yona and Little Foot, QUICKLY DRIVE OFF.

Jack's PLAN is now clear, as SILENTLY, he follows the Security Man into the DARKNESS . . .

INSIDE THE KITUWAH SCHOOL HALLWAY

Trish, Doe Angel and Awinita are about to ENTER Awinita's office again, as Doe Angel suddenly reaches out and GRABS the DIARY from Awinita.

Doe is still angry and frustrated. . .

"This is all too weird, Awinita! We're leaving.

And we're taking this DIARY back to the Station where Chief Vann and Black Hawk can help us clear this up."

Awinita releases it without resistance, knowing Chief Yona's Security man is outside, waiting for them in the School Parking Lot. . .

(SHE SPEAKS TO DOE IN THE CHEROKEE LANGUAGE)

"Go then, Little One, but remember, OUR Story must stay with the Tribe, not outsiders.

THE SHAMAN WOLFE has powerful energies over this DIARY, so be careful WHO you TRUST and WHAT you SAY."

Doe Angel stuffs the DIARY into her purse - turns to Trish without any response to Awinita, then together they march away down the long HALLWAY toward the FRONT ENTRANCE.

THE KITUWAH SCHOOL PARKING LOT

Jack quickly moves in behind the large Casino Security Man pacing him SILENTLY from behind, He FIRES a massive tranquilizer dart directly into the MAN'S soft butt tissue, just as he reaches the rear bed of Doe Angel's Pick-Up Truck.

The MAN turns in shock, surprised, then FACE PLANTS into the asphalt lot.

Jack places nylon restraints on his wrists and ankles - carefully sealing his mouth with tape - belts him securely onto Doe's truck rear bed, then moves cautiously to his own SUV.

Chapter 16

ANDERSON'S WARNING

INSIDE JACK'S MURDERED-OUT SUV

Jack quickly changes out of CAMMO, cranks the SUV and LAUNCHES the NAS NAV SYSTEM

SUDDENLY,

ON Jack, THEN ON NAS NAV SCREEN, we see Yuan's face on-screen, to Jack.

"This is MONARCH - STATUS, NAV-ONE, STATUS, NAV-ONE! **DON'T CODE-IN**"

(Yuan's actions are urgent)

"RUSH! GOTO - LIVE ENCODER, NOW!"

Jack's reaction is confusion and surprise as he reaches under his seat and releases a DEVICE - It's an encrypted ALSOS SAT PHONE - He punches in his CODE,

THEN,

Jack watches Yuan on screen. . .

"What the HELL is going on, Yuan"

Jack is very concerned.

"I'm in DEEP SHIT, DOWN HERE!"

Yuan finally speaks, his face is contorted on screen.

"We're in DEEPER SHIT, Up HERE!

Anderson took the CITATION -

He's got two Operatives and a PILOT They're at KRHP MURPHY in an hour. And Jack, they're OUT FOR BLOOD. . .

YOUR BLOOD, Jack!"

Jack carefully again watches Yuan on screen, for what's real.

"What's his problem, Yuan?"

"He's PISSED, Jack!

Thinks you've gone ROGUE!"

Jack knows what's eating Anderson, but keeps it silent.

"You know, that's NOT TRUE!"

As Yuan, spits it out clearly.

"I know that, but he doesn't - It's that MISSION in MEXICO,

He's still convinced you FUCKED UP. About the way it was RUN. . .

You know, that GIRL that got away! He thinks you're SOFT when it comes to HOT CHICKS and BOOZE, Jack!

So once again, what he's seen and heard with the NAS NAV SYSTEM on that REPORTER of yours, has set him OFF, Jack!

I could feel it when he left!"

"That's BULLSHIT! You know that, Yuan. . .

You and I have worked this system for years,

I covered your ass and you covered mine!"

"Look, Jack . . .

Anderson's got bigger problems. And we haven't got much time!"

"Neither have I, Yuan - Gotta Go!"

Jack SPIES Trish and Doe Angel EMERGING from the SCHOOL BUILDING - they're HEADING his way.

"Wait One, Yuan -

No, make that 'SHORT SIGN OFF'!"

OUTSIDE JACK'S MURDERED-OUT SUV

Jack REPLACES the LIVE SAT PHONE under his seat, then EXITS the SUV. . .

AS

Trish and Doe Angel are now RUNNING towards the SUV with what appears to be violent energy - Trish reaches him first, as she let's go pissed and shouting. . .

"Where the HELL have you been, Jack!

Some emergency BEACON this thing is!"

(She's pointing the pager at him and shaking)

"We were scared to death . . .

And waiting for YOU to save us!"

Jack shouts back at them URGENTLY STERN.

"STOP IT, you two!

We're all in serious, DEEP SHIT! FOLLOW ME!"

Jack immediately parades over to Doe Angel's Pick-up TRUCK INDICATING they should SEE into the truck bed. . .

AS

Once there, they all peer in and see the Casino Security Man BOUND with POLICE TIES in a FETAL position. He's comatose with EYES rolled back in his HEAD. . .

Doe does a quick 'WAR PRANCE', as she begins gloating.

"Damn! That's some MAJOR CRAP, Jack!"

Then she turns to Trish. . .

"Look at that, Trish!"

Then Trish reacts. . .

. . .What happened?"

Jack still STERN and very serious.

"Don't have time to explain, BABES! You'll just have to TRUST Me!

Especially YOU, Trish!!"

"Doe Angel, take Trish to the QUALLA POLICE STATION and LOCK this Guy up!

Then, find Black Hawk and get Chief Vann to set up a secure Perimeter around the Station!

They are coming for you BOTH, and this Awinita is a part of their conspiracy, along with Chief Yona and maybe the entire Qualla Council. . .

You two, and that DIARY, Are in mortal danger!"

Without their response, Jack RUSHES back to his SUV and disappears inside

BOTH Trish and Doe Angel STARE, FROZEN in a TRANCE of amazement, as he melts into the DARKNESS . . .

INSIDE JACK'S SUV

Jack again grabs the SAT PHONE initiates and MOUNTS it in a DASH holder, HEADLIGHTS ON, then CRUSHES the gas pedal - tires ripping out of the LOT and wildly pushing the SUV into the BLACK NIGHT BEYOND.

Again, Jack watches for Yuan's face.

"Are you there?" (Jack's, driving hard)

"I'm back in control . . ."

(Jack, sees Yuan on-screen)

"So, what's up, now?"

Yuan spills the dramatic end for General Anderson and the WASHINGTON TEAM to Jack, without edits.

"Macabe has Monitored Anderson's ACTIONS all along -

After all these messy incidents Anderson has sanctioned, and the FIRE STORM of LOCAL & NATIONAL NEWS MEDIA problems we're gonna be dealing with in TENNESSEE and NORTH CAROLINA, Macabe needs a convenient PATSY!

So, we're CLOSING it UP, Jack - We're SHUTTING DOWN!

Macabe wants D.C. OPS VAPORIZED! And he, wants you ON BOARD AGAIN, Jack!

YOUR NEW TARGET - Anderson, TERMINATE him and his MISSION with PREJUDICE!"

Jack merges off the INTERSTATE onto Murphy Hwy.

"HOLY SHIT! THAT'S HEAVY, Yuan!"

(Jack driving hard)

"SO, WHAT ABOUT **ALSOS**?"

(On-Screen, Yuan finger cuts his throat)

"So, THAT'S IT, Yuan!"

Yuan coughs loudly, then looks around the ROOM.

"Macabe's MOVING most of us, back to COULEE HQ.

ALSOS IS DEAD - for ALL INTENTS. . . TOO MUCH BAGGAGE -

WE'RE NOW, **O-R-I-O-N**!"

(Yuan yields a slight smirk)

"AND Jack, you can RUN your end!

Just CLEAN Anderson OUT . . .

Plus, all his Collaterals!

OH, and Jack,

MAKE that CITATION go away too. . . it's an **ALSOS** RELIC!

In fact, MACABE wants all, ASSETS tied to **ALSOS**, TO DISAPPEAR!"

Chapter 17

THE CITATION XLS

SAME TIME - MOUNTAIN VALLEYS WEST OF CHEROKEE

A DARK cloudless sky provides the CITATION XLS a perfect view down into the Mountain Valleys West of Cherokee, as the ALSOS PILOT maneuvers his JET into position for landing at KRHP MURPHY Airport.

They are lucky. The lifting FOG in the local river channel has not yet built up enough water vapor, to form clouds obstructing the RUNWAY.

The CITATION makes an observation pass at eight-thousand feet. . .

Then a nearly silent FLYBY, as the twin Pratt & Whitney PW545C high bypass engines, whine effortlessly, pushing the JET into position.

ONLY a very experienced PILOT would attempt LANDING here at NIGHT, much less in a Moonless sky. But this Pilot has those skills, as HE begins a gradual circle, then levels off to touch down from the SOUTH EAST.

A BLACK Medium sized SUV is waiting, as three suited figures depart the Jet near a hanger, then enter the vehicle.

In moments, the SUV turns onto the MAIN Highway 74, which slowly starts upward to the Robbinsville cutoff, then begins curving viciously down through the deep chasms and sharp drop-offs of the NANTAHALA GORGE, finally ending in the CHEROKEE NATION.

JACK'S SUV - DRIVING FAST

Jack is pushing hard on Highway 74, like a BAT-OUT-OF-HELL from the opposite direction, upward through the lower NANTAHALA GORGE and onward to his TARGETS.

No one is on the ROAD.

He again CODES-IN on his SAT PHONE and ACTIVATES the SUV's NIGHTVISION - then switches to BLACK-OUT DRIVING MODE.

OUR VIEW IS ON JACK, RUNNING HIGHWAY 74 and THE NAS NAV

Jack is back on the NAV screen,

AS

"OKAY, Yuan!"

(Jack's driving hard up the Mountain)

"HOW LONG - before my **ALSOS** software, cuts out?"

On the NAS NAV Screen, Yuan is urgently working his keyboard.

"YOU have three Minutes, Jack, we go BLACK in three. . .

OVER!"

Jack looks back at the Highway flashing by. . .

"CLEAR"

"Where are they now, Yuan!"

"Six miles ahead, and closing fast, Jack!"

(Jack's ready)

"What happens when we GO DARK, Yuan!"

Yuan intense and waiting. . .

"NAV'S OKAY, BUT YOUR NAS System will go BLANK,

But Any previous GPS locations Will remain STORED in the NAV."

Jack switches to glare-free windshield MODE.

"GOT IT!"

Going ACTIVE, YUAN!

GOTTA MANEUVER this BITCH.

OUT!"

Jack sees the BLACK Medium sized SUV. Headlights on HIGH BEAMS blasting his way.

BOTH SUV's are approaching a narrow zone, FAST, but they can't see him yet, he's in blackout.

NO ROAD SHOULDERS and a massive DROP-OFF on Jack's right, down into the rushing white water of the NANTAHALA RIVER, five-hundred feet below

AS

HE SLOWS, then perfectly executes a 180 DEGREE REVERSE, GUNS the GAS and immediately RAMS the smaller SUV -

He can almost HEAR their screams, as the SMALLER SUV FLOATS OFF the CLIFF into the BLACK ABYSS of the VALLEY below. . .

EVERYTHING seems to revert to SLOW MOTION.

Jack VIOLENTLY BRAKES his own SUV to keep from going over the EDGE and STOPS.

JACK'S SUV - CLIFF EDGE

Jack JUMPS out of his VEHICLE.

WE HAVE A WIDE POV ON THE CRASH SCENE,

AS

FLAMES begin erupting from the SUV, then it SMACKS DOWN THE ROCKY CLIFF into some stone fragments the near RIVER'S edge, and finally comes to REST at a LARGE BOULDER in the RIVER.

HOLDING a MAC-10 with SUPPRESSOR and SCOPE to his EYE, Jack SCANS the BURNING wreckage for MOVEMENT. NOTHING. . .

THEN HE SEES SOMETHING.

SOMEHOW, SOMEONE has survived and crawled out.

HE'S DAZED, LOOKING back up the escarpment at Jack. . .

It's Anderson gasping for air, then shouts loudly. . .

"I KNOW IT'S YOU, Jack!"

Anderson makes a final remark as he stares at Jack.

"JA'AACK, YOU MAGNIFICENT BASTARD!"

Jack SCOPES THE MAC-10 on the CENTER of ANDERSON'S CHEST - IT'S QUICK,

TWO HIGH EXPLOSIVE 45 CAL ROUNDS, BURST OUT AS THE MAN'S CHEST EXPLODES -

HIS BODY COLLAPSES INTO the rushing water of the RIVER NO OTHER SIGNS OF LIFE ARE INDICATED. . .

AS

Jack Wolcott, with inward silent satisfaction, RE-ENTERS the BLACK SUV, then RUSHES AWAY into DARKNESS.

JUST BEFORE DAWN - WE SEE JACK'S SUV DRIVING HARD

He's maneuvering FAST up the roughly paved and winding gravel roads above. . .

FONTANA LAKE.

UNTIL, AT LAST WE REACH . . .

THE SHAMAN'S RUNDOWN CABIN.

JACK'S BLACKED-OUT SUV ARRIVES, then REVERSES, backing up to the LARGE WOOD ENTRANCE DOOR

AS

Jack EMERGES with a FLASHLIGHT and lock-pick tool, WORKS the DOOR, THEN ENTERS the CABIN INTERIOR.

Jack POINTS HIS FLASHLIGHT BEAM at the CHEST OF DRAWERS

MOVES it aside and lifts the TRAP DOOR to VIEW the BANK VAULT mounted below the floor boards.

ENTERING THE COMBINATION, Jack QUICKLY OPENS IT, then picks the lock of the SOLID STEEL DOOR beneath.

ACCESSING the metal door, HE POINTS the LIGHT BEAM IN

AS

WE FINALLY SEE INSIDE THE SAFE. . .

JACK'S FACE IS AMAZED.

THE DAZZLING GLARE of GOLD BULLION BARS stacked perfectly, GREETS HIS EYES.

WITHOUT DELAY, HE PULLS out two nylon bags from his waist band and begins loading BULLION BARS, returning to LOAD the SUV several times.

After some time, Jack OPENS the SUV DRIVER'S DOOR, CHECKS a real time VEHICLE WEIGHT INDICATOR DIAL.

THE INDICATOR READS THE SUV'S AT FULL LOAD –

ONE-THOUSAND POUNDS, PLUS THE VEHICLE WEIGHT.

Then, Jack RETURNS THE CABIN SITE TO ITS ORIGINAL STATE.

LATE MORNING – THE SUV: HEADING TO MURPHY

Jack is again pushing hard, driving back South WEST along Highway 74 and the upper NANTAHALA GORGE, but the SUV LOADED, drives sluggish.

FINALLY, HE enters the VALLEY near the MURPHY AIRPORT.

HE CODES-IN on his 'SAT PHONE' to reach MONARCH.

Jack urgently keeps calling out. . .

"MONARCH, MONARCH!

COME BACK, MONARCH!"

NO RESPONSE and he knows the NAS NAV Screen is DOWN - ONLY the SAT PHONE is working.

THEN AGAIN, he urgently tries to reach Yuan

"Yuan, Yuan!

AGAIN, COME BACK, Yuan!"

SUDDENLY the line CRACKLES back to life with SOUNDS, AS - Yuan surprised he's back. . .

"COPY, Jack!

It's me, Yuan,

What's your STATUS, Jack?"

Jack at last relaxes. . .

"EXHAUSTED, Yuan! But all TARGETS TERMINATED!

You Gotta get me OUTTA HERE!

CLEAR ME, to take the CITATION!"

"Are YOU Flying yourself, Jack? Do you need the old **ALSOS** PILOT?"

"Better keep him OUT OF SIGHT, Yuan. I can fly the CITATION, Myself!"

Then Jack adds instructions to his message to Yuan. . .

"Have him TOP-OFF the Tanks, Park it in a SECURE HANGER, then place him, OFF DUTY . . .

Suggest he go to the CASINO RESORT for some R&R, maybe!

I just need him OUT OF THE WAY, ASAP!"

"OKAY, Jack?

Consider it DONE! Give me, say, forty minutes."

Jack comes back serious. . .

"Forty minutes, but that's ALL! Then, I'm outta here!"

"GOT IT, Jack! Good Luck!

 CLEAR!"

Jack adds another thought again serious. . .

"Oh, and Yuan, regardless of what happens from here on, or WHAT you hear about me, I want you on MY TEAM!

That's PERSONAL, too Yuan,

I'll always want you at my SIX!"

"THAT goes for ME TOO, Jack!

No matter how this ENDS, we'll be on the same TEAM!

Zhù hao yùn (Good Luck), Brother!

OUT!"

INTERIOR SECURE HANGER - KRHP MURPHY AIRPORT -

It's HOUR LATER and NO ONE'S AROUND AS . . .

Jack LOADs his ONE-THOUSAND POUNDS of BULLION BARS himself, from the SUV into the BAGGAGE COMPARTMENTS of the CITATION XLS.

As he finishes up, he does a COMPLETE SYSTEMS CHECK of the AIRCRAFT, Then LOCKS it up and DRIVES the SUV out of the HANGER.

EXTERIOR HANGER - KRHP MURPHY AIRPORT

Jack PULLS THE SUV into a parking place beside the FLIGHT SERVICES BUILDING at KRHP MURPHY and ENTERS, without drawing too much attention from a few workers nearby.

He's Filing his (Fake)flight plan, we observe him talking INDISTINGUISHABLY with a YOUNG WOMAN,

They're the ONLY people inside the FAA OFFICE.

In a few moments, Jack EXITS and LOOKS at his PAGER RECEIVER - URGENTLY it's BLINKING a SILENT ALARM from Trish's PAGER -

WITHOUT RESPONDING, Jack RE-ENTERS his SUV CRANKS IT, then RAMPS onto HWY 74,

Once again, in the DIRECTION of CHEROKEE.

Chapter 18

THE RECKONING

LATE MORNING - THE CHEROKEE POLICE STATION - CHEROKEE, NC

JACK'S BLACKED-OUT CHEVY SUV slowly pulls into the PARKING LOT AREA,

AS

A CHEROKEE POLICE OFFICER WALKS UP and STOPS THE VEHICLE for a SECURITY CHECK.

Jack FLASHES AN FBI AGENT ID and the OFFICER WAVES him through,

HE then EXITS the SUV and ENTERS the POLICE STATION.

EVERYTHING SEEMS CHAOTIC - OFFICERS AT DESKS WORKING - TV's blaring LOCAL and NATIONAL NEWS of the ASHEVILLE COURT HOUSE EXPLOSION - NO ONE SEEMS TO NOTICE HIM as he scans the ROOM. . .

SUDDENLY, Trish RUSHES down the corridor to Jack - HER EYES RED with tears and anguish, as SHE GRABS and HUGS HIM. . .

THEN LOOKS UP, TO FACE HIM -

Trish emotional and seriously upset. . .

"Damn it, Jack,

Where have you been!

Gabby's 'DEAD' in ASHEVILLE - And 'Larry's DEAD' in MARYVILLE!

What the HELL is going on?"

Jack deflects her pain, he's serious again.

"And where's Doe Angel, Trish?

Trish is shocked and frustrated, he's not emotional, it's like he knew this all along.

"She's in his OFFICE. . .

The Chief's OFFICE!

Jack, did you NOT HEAR what I just said!

Two of my FRIENDS are DEAD!"

Jack seizes her, looks in her EYES, then speaks softly. . .

"I got that, Trish, but you've got to calm down!

And we need to talk privately, NOW!"

Trish gets her breath, faces him. . .

"Okay, Okay . . . Where?"

Jack looks back to the ENTRANCE door.

"The SUV. . . it's just Outside."

(Jack, takes her hand)

"Come with me, Trish."

THE SUV - CHEROKEE POLICE STATION

Again, no one appears to notice them,

AS

Jack WALKS out with Trish to the BLACKED-OUT CHEVY SUV OPENS the door for her, then ENTERS the SUV himself.

Trish SLIDES CLOSE TO Jack, then KISSES him SENSUOUSLY as he GRABS her tight with the same PASSION that he had that last night in her HIGH ROLLERS SUITE.

Trish is once again hot for his body.

"Oh, GAWD, Jack, I've needed this!"

She's kissing him voraciously, then stops.

"Why, did you leave me there?

And where did you go, anyhow!"

Jack looks deep into her EYES, hoping for empathy or at least her understanding, as he begins his ultimate reveal.

"I'm not, who, you think I am, Trish - My name's not ANDERS - it's Wolcott . . . Jack Wolcott!

Trish seems frozen with shock and fear, as she awaits what he is about to say. Her doubts creep in . . .

AS

"What do you mean, Jack!"

Jack is at a loss for exactly how to say it, but he knows he must be honest, but frank. . .

"I work for a GOVERNMENT AGENCY, Trish.

It's so damn SECRET, that they KILL people, just for KNOWING about it, or what we do.

Now Trish is really petrified as she watches his face carefully.

"Oh Jack, what are you telling me!"

Jack again pleads with his EYES. . .

"I'm telling you this, Trish, Because, YOU'VE REALLY GOT ME. . .

Never before, have I felt this way.

(there's long pause)

But there's a PROBLEM, A serious PROBLEM

One, that I didn't EXPECT. . .

That 'SECRET GOVERNMENT AGENCY' -

They've SHUT IT DOWN . . .

And now for the first time in many years. . .

I'm free to get out, Go ANYWHERE.

(another long pause)

Before they try to pull me BACK IN, To something even more SINISTER."

Trish is trying to rationalize what she's hearing, she's trying to believe him, but she's terrified of where it will take her. . .

"What does this, REALLY MEAN, Jack!"

Jack finally realizes what she needs for him to clearly say.

"IT MEANS, I want you to come away with me. . ." (long pause)

"I'll help you finish your STORY, All the FACTS, NO BULLSHIT,

Then Once you're ready. . .

I've got a place deep in the CARIBBEAN for us to escape to, with plenty of money and an incredible villa on the ocean with all the amenities you could ever want. . .

(He pauses again, for her facial reaction)

If it works out for you, you'll stay, but if not, you can return to your career and KNOXVILLE . . . That's it, Trish."

WE LOOK AT JACK'S FACE THEN TRISH'S EYES

Trish seems to GAZE OFF - IMAGINING some place in the SOUTHERN CARIBE Islands, a posh resort VILLA, OVERLOOKING the bleached white sands of an endless BEACH, ULTRAMARINE crystal seas, AZURE SKIES. . .

Suddenly, HER mind enters reality again. . .

AS

SHE SLIDES closer to Jack.

She's sucked into this incredible dream with Jack. . .

Then, she says it out loud. . .

"OH FUCK IT, FUCK IT ALL!"

Finally, her doubts vanish as she again smiles at him.

"I've always wanted to be in a SECRET AGENCY or something like it, It TITILLATES me, Jack, and somehow in the deep recesses of my mind, I knew you were into something like that.

You TITILLATE me, Jack!"

Trish KISSES him again - even more DEEPLY than before. . .

Jack smiles back at his dream GAL . . .

"You, ARE what I've always wanted in life, Trish,

Yet I couldn't figure it out, or how to quite get to it. . .

Until Now, Until You, Trish!"

PART FOUR

Escape to Vapor

Chapter 19

FLIGHT TO PARADISE

THE CITATION XLS TAXI'S OUT FOR TAKEOFF AT KRHP MURPHY

FROM OUR OVERHEAD POV THE AFTERNOON SKY IS CLEAR

AS the CITATION XLS TAXI'S into position for TAKEOFF from KRHP MURPHY on the five-thousand-foot runway. . .

CLEARED BY THE TOWER the CITATION runs to full speed as the twin Pratt & Whitney engines, whine effortlessly pushing the JET to ROTATE, then it

rises in a beautiful ARC into the NORTHWESTERN
SMOKY Mountains.

SCANNING THE CITATION INTERIOR

Trish Freeman has a perfect view into the
Mountain Valleys West of Cherokee, her WINDOW
reflects a seductive smile on her face, while
Jack Wolcott carefully maneuvers his JET into the
blue skies toward KNOXVILLE, TENNESSEE.

At last, with Jack's TOP SECRET Information, she
can reveal her most incredible NEWS STORY with
confidence.

THE WKNX NETWORK CONTROL ROOM - KNOXVILLE -

WE PAN THE GIANT NETWORK ROOM UPPER AND LOWER

Trish walks past the DIRECTOR and the STUDIO
TECHNICAL CREW right to the MAIN NEWS DESK and
slips into the cushy anchor seat without a QUALM
- as the support team goes into motion and begins
THE INTRO MUSIC CUE.

In front of her, Trish has everything in DIGITAL
at her fingertips, as her MONITOR laptop shows
on-screen SQUARES with access to the entire
NETWORK'S field reporters at the Pentagon, at the
State Department, outside a Congressional
Oversight Committee Hearing Room reviewing Top

Secret NSA and CIA reports and lastly on the
White House lawn.

In front of her a bank of monitors and KEYBOARD
controls, the MAIN FLOOR Technical Team, a FLOOR
PRODUCER and her COPY WRITER feeding a PROMPTER
screen, with the OVERLAY of Trish's personally
researched speech.

THE CAMERA IS ON TRISH

AND THIS NEWS IS GONNA BE BIG -

AS,

Trish checks her, SELFIE MONITOR, and adjusts her
position for the MAIN CAMERA. . .

A micro FLASH of Jack's face, watching her out
there somewhere, enters her thoughts for
emotional support.

That fact energizes her even more, as her ear-pod
feeds a READY CUE, she needs to surpass
everyone's expectation. . .

CUE ONE: SPECIAL REPORT... We HEAR the MAIN
ANNOUNCER'S VOICE in WASHINGTON - He BELLOWS it
out,

MAIN ANNOUNCER'S VOICE:

"This A Special Report,

Coming from Knoxville, Tennessee and Washington
DC,

With, Trish Freeman."

CUE TWO - INSTANTLY:

Trish's VOICE fills all the NETWORK speakers

As the CAMERAS GO LIVE

It's Trish On ALL TV MONITORS, she's intense. . .

"Good Afternoon.

A Major Murder Case has been SOLVED and a SERIES of subsequent Explosions and Murders in Asheville North Carolina and Maryville, Tennessee have been directly attributed to a Major Government Agency Cover-up. . .

Funded and Hidden secretly without ANY Congressional Oversight since the Second World War."

Trish is clearly, authoritative, and compelling as she speaks.

"This Agency was named . . . **ALSOS**" (She pauses, and suddenly we trust her)

"It was originally formed to PROTECT the secrets of The Manhattan Atom-Bomb Project, but it somehow MUTATED into an International Squad of Operatives, Recruited from Freelance Mercenaries, the CIA, and U.S. as well as Foreign Military Special Forces Units.

These Men and Women were tasked deep within the Department of Energy (formerly the US Atomic Energy Commission - AEC)

ONLY by one MAN,

Major General R. G. Anderson! Their Missions were for Nuclear Espionage, Assassination Assignments including HEADS of Foreign Governments and anything and everything in between,

Just to PREVENT this agency, called **ALSOS**, from ever being EXPOSED to the LIGHT of DAY!"

In control now Trish clears her throat. . .

"Well, at long last, WE, as FREE and DEMOCRATIC CITIZENS of this REPUBLIC, NOW KNOW. . .

And this HORROR, will finally be STOPPED, for the GOOD of AMERICA!"

CUE THREE - INSTANTLY: Trish skillfully LOADS all the NETWORK feeds starting with. . .

Various MONITORS showing Graphics of Fontana Dam, the Fire on the Fourth Floor in the Asheville Court House, a Trailer Park Burning in Maryville Tennessee and finally an Indian Council Chief in Cherokee being hand-cuffed and taken into custody by Police Chief Vann.

Finally, the INTERVIEWS are displayed - quickly beginning with a General at the Pentagon. . .

A MONTAGE BEGINS OF NATIONAL NEWS 'HEADLINES', PLUS DIGITAL MEDIA AND CABLE NETWORKS:

"SECRET US ASSASSIN AGENCY FROM WWII STILL FUNDED"

"MASSIVE SECRET GOVERNMENT COVER-UP FROM WWII"

"MURDER IN CAROLINA CONNECTED TO TENNESSEE MURDERS"

"SECRET GOVERNMENT AGENCY KILLED NATIVE AMERICAN ENGINEER"

"GOLD RUSH COVER-UP DURING THE BUILDING OF FONTANA DAM"

"THOUSANDS OF DAM BUILDERS WOULD HAVE GONE TO THE GOLD RUSH"

INTERIOR OF THE CHEROKEE POLICE STATION

AS

Andrew Black Hawk and another Officer WALK in with two more COUNCIL MEMBERS, as Head Council Chief Yona, now in custody is seen being BOOKED.

A bustle of Local News Reporters and National MEDIA ARE scrambling to jockey for positions SCREAMING QUESTIONS,

AS

Chief Vann BEGINS his NEWS CONFERENCE for more answers -

LOCAL NEWS 'HEADLINES' AND VARIOUS NETWORKS DISPLAY:

"MASSIVE CHEROKEE COUNCIL EMBEZZLEMENT AND COVER-UP"

"COUNCIL CHIEF YONA TO BE IMPEACHED AND OUT OF OFFICE"

WE AT LAST FOCUS ON:

A PRIVATE CEMETERY NEAR FONTANA LAKE

A THICK MIST FILLS THE SURROUNDING VALLEY OF FONTANA LAKE -

Dark Gray clouds hang overhead -

Light rain begins to fall as A GROUP NATIVE AMERICAN MOURNERS stand holding umbrellas

IT'S THE WOLFE CLAN

SOFTLY they weep and murmur laments in the CHEROKEE LANGUAGE as they lower a white gauze wrapped corpse into THE EARTHEN GRAVE OF SHAMAN WOLFE, for the last time.

WE SEE THE COUPLE, THEN FOCUS ON THEIR RINGS

AT The front of the MOURNERS. . .

A young INDIAN WOMAN dressed in black STANDS solemnly beside her new husband, Andrew Black Hawk -

They are holding hands and her wedding RING tells the back STORY - a FOUR CARAT DIAMOND set in 24 CARAT GOLD -

As the young Indian Bride RAISES her head toward the misty sky above,

We view a satisfied FACE and beautiful EYES,

- it's Doe Angel.

Chapter 20

A VILLA ON BONAIRE

A CITATION JET SECRETLY LANDS ON THE DUTCH ISLAND OF BONAIRE

BONAIRE, CARIBE – THREE MONTHS LATER

Trish Freeman is scurrying through a fresh market on the ISLAND OF BONAIRE tasting various fruits and vegetables as SHE gathers her bags, exits the MARKET and hails a Jitney to take her home

AS they pass the small local AIRPORT, she hears the familiar whine of JET Engines and glances up at what appears to be another CITATION like Jack's, following a VECTOR for landing.

IN moments later, Trish arrives at the beautiful OCEANFRONT VILLA of CROWN ROYAL, codes in her access key and ENTERS the enclosed CAR PARKING AREA –

VILLA ENTRANCE, into the Kitchen

Trish is in a playful mood as she opens up. . .

"Jack, how are those STEAKS coming!"

Jack Wolcott is at last a very relaxed man. . .

AS

"JUST about ready, can you grab a RED, Trish?

So how was the market?"

Trish works the veggies, but she's curious. . .

"Same as usual. . .

Did see what I thought was a Citation like yours, Landing. . .

We don't see many of those down here,

Do we?"

Jack reacts casually, since all has now changed for him.

"No Kidding - They're larger than most on this Island, except for mine!"

(long pause, back to casual)

"STEAKS are DONE. . .

Let's Eat!"

VILLA GAZEBO AND POOL – NEAR SUNSET

They sit on the veranda sipping wine and enjoying each other, like true romantics in LOVE. . .

Trish pulls off her COVER-UP, exposing her sexy new yellow Victoria Secret BIKINI and playfully romps down to the beach edge

Without hesitating, SHE'S in the warm tropical sea water moving to their swim platform. Not a ripple in the water as the last light of SUNSET, glistens on the flat surface.

Trish waves to Jack. . .

"COME on in, BABE!

You can see the final SUNSET. It's a better view out here, Jack."

Jack waves back, but HE seems occupied with his CELL, as he tries to reach his HANGER OPERATIONS MAN at the AIRPORT, to confirm Trish's possible sighting of a CITATION – as HE turns back. . .

SUDDENLY Trish IS NOWHERE TO BE SEEN, AS Jack REALIZES SOMETHING'S UP –

HE RUSHES INTO the WATER, SWIMMING HARD to the PLATFORM FIRST CHECKING THE SURFACE, THEN UNDERWATER. . .

AS

A BLACK SUITED SCUBA DIVER has just fired a MIDAZOLAM fast acting Tranquillizer Dart into Trish's leg and SHE'S drifting to the shallow bottom

Jack peers under the surface and SEES Trish, then THE LONE SCUBA DIVER re-arming his DART GUN . . .

Jack GOES for HIM, BUT IT'S TOO LATE. . .

HE'S also HIT, this time in the chest, as Jack begins drifting downward, out of control, into THE ULTIMATE UNDERWATER DARKNESS. . .

OUR POV - SEA SURFACE, THEN QUICKLY BACK TOWARD THE VILLA

UNAWARE, A MAN comes out of a bathroom near the VILLA'S infinity pool drying his hands with a tropical colored beach towel.

Suddenly, he realizes NO ONE is around, anywhere!

He MOVES like lightning, opening a lower drawer at the pool side bar, then turns to the beach with a massive PISTOL.

THE MAN'S POV - SEA SURFACE, BUBBLES NEAR A CONCRETE JETTY

The MAN briefly turns to face us, it's Yuan, as he grabs a SCUBA MASK lying at pool side before rushing the beach.

He dons the Mask and silently enters the sea water SEARCHING.

Then he SEES it, the FORM of a lone scuba diver moving away under the bubbles. . .

AS

Yuan's movements underwater are as sleek as a PORPOISE

FOCUSED on the distance to his TARGET, Yuan fires the HK-P11 PISTOL

INSTANTLY the TARGET is HIT, as Yuan fires another, then another.

BLOOD detonates, obscuring our view as the DIVER'S form sinks slowly away. . .

TURNING back to the SWIM PLATFORM, Yuan dives below it and recovers Trish, placing her on the shore, then quickly returns to Jack who's located even closer to the beach.

Yuan is WORKING FEVERISHLY on Trish and Jack

AFTER intolerable minutes of mouth to mouth, resuscitation efforts, running back and forth to the lower BAR drawer for breathers, Adrenaline injectors and other Drugs, Yuan EXPLODES with JOY. . .

AS

WE HAVE A WIDE POV - BEACH SCENE WITH TRISH AND JACK

Trish, then Jack, blow off their BREATHERS and begin violent coughing. . .

SHOCKED, they look up to SEE each other, then Yuan, smiling back at them, as finally they ALL start LAUGHING.

OUR POV - From the beach, we slowly move upward to above the Villa, then higher again into puffy white clouds, then even higher over Bonaire, to a Satellite view of the lower Southern Caribbean, and at last to the Lens-Eye of a Space Camera with an Emblem and one word - **"ORION"**

- SOMEONE IS WATCHING THEM

                    THE END

Milton Keynes UK
Ingram Content Group UK Ltd.
UKHW021511250824
447344UK00016B/898